I0731349

THE RANCHER TAKES HIS RUNAWAY BRIDE

THE RANGERS OF PURPLE HEART RANCH BOOK 3

SHANAE JOHNSON

THOSE JOHNSON GIRLS

Edited by Alyssa Breck

Manufactured in the United States of America
First Edition May 2020

"*B*ut how can you be sure the beans came from Caldas, Columbia?" Lana Hunt leaned over the counter, pinning the man with what she called her penetrative gaze.

That stern gaze that told the other person that she saw more than they wanted her to was one of the skills needed to be an investigative journalist. There was a fine art to questioning a source, getting them to divulge information without them realizing they were—well—spilling the beans. When it came to information exchange, it was all about asking the right question.

For example, a reporter never asked a closed-ended question like Are these Arabica beans? The interviewee could simply answer Yes or No, and the communication channels would close.

It was best to use an open form of questioning that began with something like *Tell me about these beans*. Or, *Can you relay how you came into possession of these particular beans*? That way, the responder would feel obliged to divulge not only their knowledge but their opinion and feelings, too.

"Another question," Lana said before the bewildered barista could answer the first question.

Lana leaned over the counter, twisting the ring on her finger. The pad of her thumb pushed the small diamond around until it was at the back. Mac said she always did that when she was thinking things over. Lana doubted her fiancé's observation. She hadn't worn the ring long enough to form any habits. It had only been three months since Mac had slid it on her left hand, his brown eyes shining in triumph.

The young man standing behind the counter did not look triumphant as he gaped at Lana. Sweat trickled down his splotchy, side-burned face, and his man bun drooped. Clearly, he was feeling the pressure because he wouldn't quite meet her gaze. He stared, instead, over her shoulder.

Great. She was close to cracking him. Lana placed both her hands on the counter and cocked her head as she went in for the kill. Dogged determination was yet another hallmark of the investigative journalist.

"I happen to know that true Arabica beans are a deep reddish-purple and smell sweet like jasmine flowers."

Research skills were another hallmark of investigative reporting. Lana had studied her material. She inhaled, ready to fire her next missive when she smelled a delicate, flowery smell. Like jasmine. She glanced down at the dark, nearly purple beans.

"All's I know is what it says on the packaging," said the side-burned barista.

Lana looked behind the counter to see an industrial-sized brown container with the words *Arabica Beans* printed on the side. As far as facts went, that one was hard to argue with.

"Come on, lady," called a disgruntled voice behind her. "Take your order and go. Some of us have to get to work."

Lana tapped her credit card on the coffee shop's machine. She declined when it asked if she wanted to leave a tip. Since the barista hadn't given her a tip she might've used to create a news story for her job, she wouldn't return the favor of tipping him for his. Grabbing hold of the tray of coffees, Lana made her way out of the mom and pop coffee shop and into the warm air.

She noticed the world all around her. She might not have gotten what she needed for an exposé on coffee shops passing off inferior beans. But there were still potential stories all around her, all just waiting to be told.

A man walked out of a bank with a locked briefcase clutched in his hand. He looked left, right, and then clutched the satchel tighter. What, Lana wondered, could he be hiding in the bowels of that case?

A young mother pushed a stroller toward the park. She paused to allow a fit jogger to pass her. But when the young, athletic man did, she craned her neck over her shoulder to get a view of him passing. Could there be trouble at home, Lana wondered?

Unfortunately, those potential stories would have to wait a little longer because Lana was late for work.

She dashed into her car, settling the coffee into the passenger seat. Ten minutes later, with one minute to spare, she was riding the elevator up to the third floor of *ChatterZine*. People bustled about inside of the online magazine. The red ink flowed down white sheets of paper as copy was edited. The slicing sound of scissors cut through the air as images were pasted and rearranged for the layout. Interns scuttled and scurried about checking facts, running copies, and getting coffee for their assigned reporters.

With aromatic coffee in hand, Lana made her way to *ChatterZine*'s Editor in Chief's office. Reyanna Murphy didn't raise her head when Lana opened the door. Not until the swirling tendrils of warm coffee rose in the air and tickled her nose.

"Arabica beans?"

Lana nodded. "I checked the sources myself."

Reyanna took a healthy gulp. The brown skin of her throat that matched the beans she loved worked as she took in the warm nectar that she worshipped. "Thanks, kid."

Lana wasn't a kid. She was twenty-two. But she didn't check her boss's facts. Initiative was another highly prized skill for an investigative reporter. She just needed Reyanna to take a glance away from the energizing morning brew and see the same fire in her intern.

"Did you finish fact-checking Nichols's story?" asked Reyanna after another sip.

"I finished last night."

It had taken Lana into the evening, well after she should've left the office and gone home. There had been a lot of errors in Nichols's story; factual and grammatical. Lana had practically rewritten the story before she turned it in. She wanted to tell Reyanna that, but Lana suspected the woman knew.

So, why hadn't Reyanna given Lana her own story to write instead of another's to rewrite?

"Andrew Rucker is out again." Reyanna sighed as she gripped her coffee to her chest.

"I hope it's nothing serious." Lana knew full well that the man was likely sleeping off yet another night of illicit delights.

"I'm trying to find something to fill his section."

Another part of investigative journalism was being cutthroat. This was it. This was her chance. "I have an idea for a story."

Reyanna studied her over the rim of her coffee cup. "Your fact-checking has been stellar. I've noticed both Nichols's and Rucker's stories have been... tighter."

Lana smiled demurely, admitting nothing.

"Yes." Reyanna gave a decisive nod. "I think you can handle this story."

Inwardly, Lana jumped up and down. Outwardly, she took a seat across from her boss. She set her mind to determine which story to pitch. An exposé on coffee shops might pique Reyanna's interest, but Lana had no angle. Maybe an investigation into the security of briefcases. Or an exploration of the satisfaction of today's young mothers in the roles as homemaker and wife.

"There's this woman in the next town over," Reyanna started. "She has twenty cats and—"

"Don't tell me," Lana said, taking out the pen she always tucked into her hair and the notepad that was always in her back pocket. "Animal control is on her?"

"No," said Reyanna. "She makes the cats costumes."

"Oh, I see. So, it's an animal cruelty angle."

"No, Lana. It's a fluff piece about a woman with cats who puts them in funny costumes."

Lana's pen lowered. She sat the blank notepad down on her lap as she struggled to understand the straight lines of the story.

"I want you to go and ask some basic questions,

take pictures—lots of pictures. Everyone loves a cat photo."

A fluff piece about cats in costumes? Not an exposé on code violations or a treatise on the plight of today's aging, single woman. Or even a statement piece on how modern feminism is owning a cat.

"Can you handle that?" asked Reyanna.

"Yes." Lana cleared her throat. "Yes, I can."

"Excellent. You can go and interview her on Friday."

"This Friday?" Lana shifted the pen in her hand and twisted the ring on her finger. The diamond met with the ink of the pen.

"Yes, we need the story for the weekend edition."

"This weekend?" Lana twisted the ring the other way, this time meeting the edge of the notepad in her lap.

Reyanna lifted her gaze. "Is there a problem?"

Lana moved the ring up and down, toward her knuckle and then back all the way down. Yes, there was a problem. She had a bit of a family obligation this Saturday.

"No." With one final press of her thumb, Lana shoved the ring firmly back in place. "There's no problem. I just have this family thing. But I can probably wiggle out of it. Or get them to push it back."

"Good. I'm counting on you."

Mac was not going to be happy. But he loved her. Enough to marry her. They were going to spend the rest of their lives together. He couldn't get mad if she wanted to push the start of that forever back by one weekend. Not when it meant she would get a step closer to her dream job.

CHAPTER TWO

*M*ac Kenzie looked himself over in the full-length mirror. He looked mighty fine if he did say so himself. If ever he was going to do so, he was going to look good enough to break all the girls' hearts, he'd do it in this suit. His wedding tuxedo.

Not that he had any intentions of breaking any girls' hearts. Mac had fallen head over heels in love with Lana Hunt the first time he'd seen her. The first time he'd seen her had been just over there.

Mac turned to look out the window of his childhood bedroom. Well, his summertime childhood bedroom. As a kid, Mac had rarely lived in the same place for more than a few months at a time. With two parents in different branches of the

Armed Forces, Mac had been shuttled from base to base and had even spent a couple of years in boarding school while his parents fulfilled their duty to the country.

The only thing that had a semblance of normalcy was his summers, which he spent there, at his grandparent's house. He'd spent every summer there since he was six. His fiancée, Lana, had done the same. She came every summer to stay with her grandparents, who lived next door. Lana's bedroom was directly across from his.

The sun had set. The neighborhood was quiet. The lights of her bedroom were out this evening. She was probably staying late at work. Again.

Mac heaved a sigh as he straightened his tie. He knew he was marrying an ambitious woman. He loved that about his Lana; that she had a single-minded focus. It had taken him years to break through that focus to get her to look up from her newspaper articles and magazine columns. It had taken him even more years to get her to see him as more than a friend.

After much prodding, poking, cajoling, and convincing, she had. The proof was in the ring she'd finally accepted from him. It had only taken him a mere five times in asking. In just a couple of days, she would finally be his forever. Not just for the summers they spent together. They'd be together every day for the rest of their lives.

Without warning, a hand shot over the barrier of the open window sill. Mac jolted. Not from seeing the hand there. He was used to that. Ever since they'd been children, Lana had often climbed into his bedroom window for a late-night chat. It was such an old habit that even now, they both neglected to use the front door of the houses.

But Lana climbing into his window on this night, at this particular time, was his worst nightmare about to come true.

"Lana, no."

Mac grabbed the patchwork quilt his grandfather had knitted him from the bottom of the bed. To work his arthritic fingers, his retired Air Force pilot grandad had taken up the hobby and was quite proud of his work. Mac threw the intricate artwork over his covered body.

"You can't see me like this."

Lana easily stepped over the window sill and into the room. She was dressed in dark pants and a bright blouse. Pants that were now scuffed from her climb and a shirt that held a hint of dampness at the armpits for her efforts. Lana wasn't one of those women that cared for messing up clothes. Clothing was just armor to her, a tool to help her get the job done.

Dark blue eyes narrowed at Mac as she came to standing. She shoved the black tresses out of her angular face to peer up at him. "I can't see you like what?"

"I'm in my wedding tux." Mac tugged the edges of the quilt tighter around himself. "It's bad luck for you to see me like this."

Lana quirked one of her dark brows. "Isn't that myth about the bride in her wedding gown?"

Mac pursed his lips, still not letting go of the quilt. "I'm sure it goes both ways."

"I don't care about that." Lana took a step toward him.

Mac stepped back. Which was entirely counterintuitive. For more than half his life, Mac had been chasing after this girl, trying to capture her into his arms.

"I need to talk to you. Mac, if you're so bothered, just take it off."

Mac lifted a brow at that. He might've spent the last three months wrapped up in planning their wedding, but he'd spent more than enough hours making an agenda for their wedding night. He only had a few more days before he'd see Lana in her wedding dress, and then help her out of it.

As if she saw the trajectory of his thoughts, Lana huffed at him. More than once, she'd accused him of not taking things seriously. She was wrong. He took his vows to her very seriously.

At age six, Mac had vowed they'd be best friends forever.

At twelve, he vowed that he would have his first kiss with Lana.

At age seventeen, Mac had sworn he would marry Lana.

It had taken time, but he'd kept each and every one of those vows. All that was left was the vows he'd prepared as they officially began their lives together. Starting this weekend.

But first, he had to make sure nothing got in the way of the perfect wedding he'd planned for them. And that started with the bride not seeing the groom in his wedding clothes.

Mac made a twirling motion with his index finger, indicating that Lana should turn around. With a huff, she did as he asked. That was the first thing that alerted Mac that whatever she came to tell him might be serious. Lana had always done as she pleased. She was a woman that knew her own mind.

Mac grinned and shed the tuxedo jacket and shirt. At the last minute, he shoved a fatigue shirt from his days in basic training over his head. Now that the woman of his dreams had finally said yes, he would be separating from the military. He hated to leave behind his Army Ranger friends, but Lana had always been his first priority.

Mac came up behind his fiancée. She settled back into his arms as he slid his hands around her. A sense of rightness lightened his heart as he buried his nose in her hair.

"How was your day at the office, honey?" he said.

"It was good." Lana rested her hands over his. With her left thumb, she twisted her engagement ring around. "I got a story assignment."

Mac whirled her around. "That is amazing. I knew you could do it."

Lana let him pull her into his chest, she snuggled in under his chin at the spot he'd told her was meant only for her. "It's a fluff piece. But it's my chance."

"You're going to nail it."

Mac pulled away. Peering down at her, he saw a light in her blue eyes. He brushed his lips over hers, reveling in the bittersweet taste of her. Coffee and cream, that was his reporter girl.

"I suppose you'll want to work on the story on

our honeymoon." Mac sighed, pulling her more snuggly into him. "Fine, but only a few hours. I want most of your time and attention."

"About that..."

Lana squirmed away and out of his hold. She flicked at the ring when she was away from him. Mac felt a prickle of foreboding slither down his spine. She only flicked at her ring when she was unsure of something, which had been every time she'd been asked her opinion on anything to do with their wedding planning.

Lana's indecision and disinterest in the planning hadn't bothered Mac. He'd happily, daresay eagerly, picked up all the slack that was traditionally set for the bride. After all, he was the one who'd been dreaming about this day since they were kids.

"About what?" Mac prodded her.

"About the wedding..."

The shiver that had gone down his spine transformed into a tingle of awareness. Mac didn't think Lana was backing out of the wedding. Though he was the only one who believed they'd ever get close to this day. His friends hadn't even bought plane tickets until just a couple of weeks ago. His parents had scheduled a vacation around the date, just in case.

In truth, Lana had taken a long time to say yes to the engagement. He'd asked her five times over the last two years. But it had taken her three years before she'd agreed to date him. So, there was a marked improvement.

"The interview for my story is scheduled for Friday." Lana shoved the ring up to her knuckle.

"This Friday? Our wedding day?"

She nodded, rubbing at the band around her finger. "I was thinking we could just push the ceremony back a couple of hours."

"Push our wedding ceremony back?"

Lana shoved the ring back down. "Yeah, it could be in the evening instead of the morning. I'll just head out, do the interview, and be back in plenty of time to say *I do*."

Mac's head was spinning as he looked at her. She hadn't taken the ring off. That should soothe him. But it didn't. What had his blood boiling was the change request.

It wasn't the first time she'd asked to push the date back. And each date shift had been due to her work. She'd missed most of the planning appointments because she'd chosen to stay late or follow a lead for her work. Mac hadn't begrudged her until now.

"An evening wedding?" Mac tried not to spit out the words, but they were so distasteful on his tongue. "I planned for an afternoon wedding. The hall is booked. The band, the caterers. Do you know how many people have been invited?"

Just a few dozen of their closest family and friends. Mac had addressed each invitation himself. Lana had been working late that night, fact-checking some story about the dangers lurking in nail salon foot baths.

"I told you not to go through all that trouble," she said. "You're the one that wanted the big wedding. We could've gone to Vegas months ago and got this over with."

"Over with?" Mac nearly choked. "I planned all of this for you."

"No. You did this for you," she said. "What difference does it make when and where we get married?"

"Every difference. We planned this."

"No, actually, you planned this. You want the purple and pink colors—"

"Plum and blush."

"And the roses—"

"Lilacs, not roses."

"And the hundreds of guests."

"It's only going to be seventy-eight. And that's only because your grandmother insisted on inviting the Wallaces from down the street."

Lana huffed. Her hands were balled into fists as she glared at him. She wasn't turning the engagement ring, but he didn't need that to interpret her feelings.

"Mac, this story is important to me."

"Lana, our wedding, which is the starting point for the rest of our lives, is important to me."

"Our life together began years ago. What difference does one day make?"

What difference?

The room was spinning. Mac took a step back, needing to find something to hold him up. Did she really just say those words?

He'd always known that Lana wasn't like the typical girl. She was laser-focused on her career goals. But she'd always made time for him. Yet, now, when he needed her most, she wanted a rain check on their wedding day?

"Look," Lana sighed, "why don't we just elope after I finish the story?"

"E—" Mac choked. He couldn't even finish the word.

"Isn't the important thing that we'll be married?" she said. "I'm just asking for another day."

Mac shook his head. "If we push this back now, next week it'll be something else. Another story. Another excuse. Either you want to spend your life with me. Or you don't."

"I do. I don't see why I can't have a career as well as a husband."

"I don't see why I can't have a wife who puts me ahead of her career."

The moment the words were out of his mouth, he knew he should regret them. Except he didn't. He'd put her happiness ahead of his career. He'd bent over backward to accommodate her choices. He'd made all the choices for this wedding. It wasn't unreasonable for him to want to keep the date.

Lana twisted the ring on her finger. It spiraled up, like a topper being uncorked. The band reached as high as her knuckle. Even in their worst arguments, she'd never lifted it over her knuckle.

Mac held his breath as the band sat at the crease of her knuckle.

Lana balled her hand into a fist. The band slipped just below her bent knuckle. But before Mac could exhale, Lana turned and walked over to the open window.

"I love you," he said before she got a leg over.

Lana turned back to him. "I love you."

This was where he would always bend to her will, agreeing to do whatever she wanted. But on this point, he was not going to budge. Either their lives started on Friday, or they'd part.

They stared at each other for long moments. Neither budging. Finally, Lana lifted her leg over the window sill.

Mac felt himself giving, but at the last second, his back remained straight. "I'll be at the church on Friday afternoon waiting for you."

Lana twisted the ring until the diamond was lost inside her fist. Then she climbed out of the window and was gone.

CHAPTER THREE

*N*ine months later

Lana rode up the elevator to the offices of *ChatterZine*. Like she did every morning, including most weekends, she gripped a cup of coffee in one hand. Though now it was only one cup as Reyanna had gone through a series of bright-eyed interns, whose eagerness dulled within weeks of working for the demanding boss.

Coffee in hand. Pen in bun. Notepad in pocket. Lana took sure steps to her desk. Along the way, she dodged bodies as writers and photographers hurried about inside the office.

As always, the red ink flowed as black copy was stricken across white sheets of paper. Scissors made quick work of photographs and illustrations as the day's layout came together like pieces of a puzzle. Unlike her first year here, this batch of interns stood on the periphery, eyeing the madness with a bit of fear in their eyes. Maybe two of them would make it in this fast-paced, unrelenting, cutthroat world of online reporting. The others would need to take a step back into the world of print.

Lana breathed it all in. This was her world. She was in her element.

So why, with the deep breath, didn't her lungs fully inflate?

Likely because everyone was always out of breath in the world of reporting. Life moved fast in the world of news. To succeed, she had to be nimble enough to catch it. Which meant holding still was for the birds. And so Lana hurried into her seat.

All around her keyboards clacked. It was Lana's favorite sound. The sound of notes being turned into stories.

Though Joe Grist, the political reporter, did jam his fingers into the keys as though his fingertips were jackhammers, and the keyboard was concrete. And

Mary James, the fashion reporter, had a habit of uncrumpling the recycled paper in the bin and peering at what others threw away as she waited by the copy machine.

Then there was the new batch of interns, still hovering at the edge of the room. They reminded Lana of old Three Stooges movies when they braved a step forward. They'd bump and bumble into one another while they got facts of the stories wrong.

Lana pulled her keyboard to herself. She hadn't assigned a single one of them one of her stories. Because she didn't have time to do double the work.

"You coming out to happy hour with us?" Warren Blake leaned over the wall of her cubicle. The sportswriter was handsome. Most of the girls in the office were fawning over him.

He kept singling Lana out. Not that she'd once given him an ounce of encouragement. He seemed to view her as though she were a ball that was up in the air waiting for him to catch.

"I can't. I've gotta finish this story." Lana pointed to the screen that held her completed piece for the week.

"I'm surprised that fiancé of yours never comes into this office and drags you away."

Lana twisted the engagement ring on her left ring finger with her thumb. "He's busy."

"Too busy to check in on his girl?"

"He can't. He's overseas. He's an Army Ranger."

"An American hero?" Warren raised a brow as though he was impressed. "Nice one."

Lana nodded in agreement. Mac was a hero and a nice one. Unlike Warren, who constantly hit on a woman who was clearly unavailable.

Well, she was technically unavailable. She hadn't shown up for her wedding. But she hadn't broken the engagement. She hadn't given the ring back. She hadn't even considered it. She fully intended to marry Mac Kenzie.

Some day.

Though she'd probably have to talk to him to determine when that day might be. Or if that day could ever be.

Mac had redeployed last fall, just a few weeks after their summer wedding had been canceled. Lana hadn't heard from him all year. Not since the night she climbed out of his bedroom window for the last time.

"I hope he knows what a lucky man he is," Warren was saying. "If you were mine, I'd sneak away to see you for lunch and happy hour."

Lana didn't answer Warren. She twisted the band on her finger. It was a comfort sitting on her hand all the nights when she wasn't in Mac's arms. When she wasn't seeing his bright smile. Or feeling his warmth as he held her close. Or listening to that deep rumble of laughter that made his whole body shake and then seeped into her and made her laugh.

She'd done what she'd done. And she had no regrets. At least that's what she told herself every night she went home alone.

This career was what she'd always dreamed of. Chasing down a story. Getting the facts out of subjects. Turning that evidence into beautifully crafted prose.

Okay, so the current story she was working on wasn't exactly Pulitzer worthy. But she was still rising to the top. She'd gone from cat stories to dog stories, and now she was actually doing human stories.

Her latest story had been on the man who held the record for the longest toenails. Along with his nightly cleaning regimen. Lana had prided herself for holding the contents of her stomach down as she interviewed the man. She'd aced that story, and she was sure more hard-hitting assignments were on the way.

"Hunt. In here."

Lana's right eye twitched at the sound of her boss's voice. She took another healthy gulp of coffee. The robust brew warmed her belly and gave her the kick of energy she needed for the day ahead. She rose and made her way to her editor's door, passing an intern who looked slightly green around the ears on the way out.

"Nichols is out sick," Reyanna started without preamble.

Too bad for poor old Nichols. Brilliant for Lana. Taking over his stories was how she was moving up in the ranks. Though Lana often wondered why her boss bothered to keep the man on the payroll if he rarely did his job.

"You finished the toenail story?"

"Of course," Lana said, tugging her pen from her bun and pulling her notebook from her back pocket. "It's in your inbox now."

Reyanna offered Lana a rare grin. "I can always count on you."

"What's the story?"

"There's a ranch in Montana where men are marrying women off left and right." Reyanna sat back, crossing her hands over her flat stomach. She'd cringed when she'd said the word *marriage*. "It's being hailed as the modern-day

Gold Rush Brides." Another cringe when she said the word *bride*.

Reyanna was unmarried and unattached. She was always in this office when Lana arrived in the morning. The editor-in-chief was still in the chair when Lana went home last each evening. The many times Lana had come in over the weekend this past year, she'd seen Reyanna behind this desk, clacking away at her computer. No wonder the idea of a relationship was foreign to the woman.

"You think it's some kind of cult?" asked Lana.

"Cult or a scam?" Reyanna shrugged. "I hear it has something to do with land ownership. Maybe government tape? The interesting angle is that all the men are soldiers."

Lana's pen scratched across the paper and drew a jagged line on the knee of her pants. She gulped a couple of times before she could speak. "What branch?"

"All of them, I think. It's a rehabilitation ranch for wounded veterans."

Lana let out the breath she held. Mac wouldn't be there. He was neither wounded nor a veteran. He wouldn't be released from the army until the summer.

For the past ten years, they'd met at their

grandparents' houses each summer. Either she would climb into his bedroom if he arrived first. Or he would climb into hers.

Lana had planned to take some time off to visit her grands in a few months when the temperature rose and the beaches opened. And if it so happened on a cool summer night that she let her window unlocked and a strapping soldier wanted to climb in, she wouldn't stop him.

Unless he didn't come back. Unless it was truly over between the two of them. Which was possible.

Mac had chased her for years. He might take a step back, but he never backed down. He never gave up each time she rebuked him or tried to slow his roll. He'd always flash that impish grin and come back at her from a different angle.

Which had been exhausting.

Which had been why Lana had backed out of the wedding.

She'd loved Mac—she loved Mac. Not past tense. He was just so determined to have his way and tug her along with him as he did so.

But what if there were no more angles? What if he'd turned and walked in a different direction? He might've even found someone else by now. A girl who wanted to have a huge wedding, and stay home, and be a happy housewife.

Lana hated that girl.

"Hunt? Do you want the marry a soldier story? Or not?"

"Yeah," Lana sighed. "Yeah, I want it."

CHAPTER FOUR

*L*ater that morning, Mac Kenzie lifted his head up and looked out at the wide Montana skyline. Blue sky blended into green pastures. Spotted along the pastures were blotches of brown blobs that were the herd of Vance Ranch, where he currently made his home.

His home was in the sweltering third-floor attic of the ranch's big house, but he'd lived in worse. He'd happily trade the deserts of Afghanistan or the mountains in Syria for the cramped, humid attic any day.

Mac took a deep inhale of the fresh, open-air, and promptly coughed as a dust cloud swirled into his nostrils. The new bull for the Vance Ranch was kicking up a storm in the pen.

It was no wonder why. The animal had gotten a glimpse of the heifers he was about to be locked into a pen with. The new bull was raring to go on his speed dating adventures.

The old bull sat with his bulk on the ground, his large head hanging low. The old bull was bigger than the new bull. But the old bull had taken a mighty blow that left him laid out on his belly. The injured creature lifted his head to glance at his replacement, then slumped back down in defeat.

Mac could relate. In the relationship department, Mac had been replaced by something he didn't view was better than himself. Mac had been replaced by something that wasn't just smaller, it wasn't even his same species.

The love of Mac's life had walked away from him in pursuit of a career.

The injured bull let out a low whine, as though to commiserate with Mac. Mac leaned against the fence in solidarity. Nearly a year later, and he could hardly still believe it himself. But here he was on a cattle ranch while Lana was likely chasing around stories to put in print. Or digital ink, or whatever.

What Mac did know was that he'd chased the love of his life relentlessly for years, and once again, she'd slipped away.

Mac stepped back into the corner as Brenda opened the latch to release the new bull into the females' pen. The females moved quickly, darting out of the way of the randy bull. They might be interested, but none were eager to get caught too soon.

The injured bull sighed again. The veterinarian had told them that cattle have a high tolerance for pain. Much higher than a human.

Mac understood that too. He wore a grin most days, while inside, he felt like his heart was in a perpetual fire that breathing only stoked.

The old bull would heal. He just needed time. Then he could get back to the work of wooing the female cattle next year.

That was Mac's plan. It was an old plan. Most of his life, he'd only get to spend summers with Lana. On the last day, they parted ways, and he had to begin his pursuit again next June.

It had been nine months since Mac's wedding day. It was the middle of spring now. In just a few more months, he'd go in search of her and win her back.

It didn't matter how long it took. Lana was the only woman for him. He'd given her time to work on her career. She had to be missing him now. If she ran again, he would bide his time a bit more. But he'd never give up on her.

A truck pulled up, snapping Mac out of his reverie. When Mac saw who was inside the vehicle, he pushed off the fence and hurried over. Three men filed out of the vehicle.

"Finally," Mac whooped.

David Porco was the first out of the vehicle. He bounded to Mac like a puppy who had been cooped up inside for too long. Which was an apt description of the man with shaggy hair and large, dark eyes.

"Mackenzie," Porco howled as he bowled into Mac.

Mac happily accepted the man's enthusiastic greeting. He was just glad it didn't come with a lolling lick of his chin.

Next was Jordan Spinelli. Spinelli reached his hand out to Mac with a smart smile and a nod. Spinelli was the scholar of the bunch who always had his head buried in tactical books.

Russell Hook came round from the driver's side. Rusty was the eldest of the bunch. But only by a few years. The gray hairs the man sported were from stress rather than time.

"We stopped off at the Purple Heart Ranch,"

Rusty said after giving Mac a clap on the back. "They told us to come over here. Have we changed properties?"

"It's a long story," said Mac.

"You three have only been here for two weeks," said Porco. "And we hear congratulations are in order? You got hitched?"

"Not me." Mac held up his hands. "Keaton and Grizz."

"So, what they say about the Purple Heart Ranch is true?" said Spinelli. "Soldiers come out here and get married."

The man looked around the rolling pastures as though single women dressed in wedding gowns were preparing to jump out at him. Crazier things had happened. Like their leader, Anthony Keaton getting hitched the same day he'd arrived here.

Mac related the story of how the old bull had rammed into Keaton's truck on his arrival. Though the bull was still laid up and suffering, the animal had knocked good sense into Keaton. He'd looked up to see Brenda Vance riding to save him on a horse, and that had been the end of it. The two married so that she could give him the land the six of them needed to complete their training camp. But

Keaton had wound up giving the female rancher his heart.

A few days later, Keaton's baby sister showed up. Grizz had been trying to deny his feelings for Patricia Keaton since the young woman had come of age. But after just a couple of days, Patty had finally sunk her claws into Grizz, and the two turned up married.

If only Lana would turn up here. That would solve all of Mac's problems.

"There's no way I'm staying here," said Spinelli. "I'm too young for a ball and chain."

"You are a ball and a chain," said Porco throwing the man a punch.

"At least you don't have to worry, Rusty. You're already married."

Spinelli had a knack for saying the wrong things at the wrong times. It wasn't that he was insensitive. His brain was often too busy working out big, complex problems that he didn't pay attention to people's feelings.

Rusty let out a low sigh. "Not for long."

No one spoke. They all knew divorce papers were in the works for Rusty and his estranged wife. The papers were signed. But the ink hadn't come from Rusty's pen.

"Come meet the new family," said Mac to break up the tense silence.

The four men went to the other side of the pen, where Keaton and Brenda were keeping an eye on the new bull. Keaton had his arm looped around his wife's shoulder. Beside them stood Patty and Grizz in a tight embrace.

When the two men looked up to see their army brothers, they each tore themselves away from their wives and came forward with open arms. Greetings were exchanged. Backs were clapped. Jabs were thrown, ducked, and counterpunched.

"We need to get you all over to the training camp and show you guys what we've done." Keaton's typically regimented tone was full of eagerness.

"I hear you've relaxed that crazy schedule," said Porco. "Thank you, Brenda."

"We're also helping Bren out here on the ranch," said Keaton. "And now, my mother is demanding a wedding for both her children."

"No worries," said Mac. "I can help with the wedding stuff."

The men all turned and looked at him. The ladies did, too. Brenda with relief in her green gaze. Patty, with doubt in her blue eyes.

"What? My grandmother was a wedding planner. Plus, I'm an evolved man. Come on, ladies."

Planning a double wedding was just what Mac needed to get his mind off his own failed wedding, as well as divert his attention from planning and hoping for what the summer might bring.

CHAPTER FIVE

*L*ana took her last sip of tepid coffee as she pulled up to the gate of the sprawling ranch. For a moment, she doubted she was in the right place. The sign on the wrought iron at the front of the establishment said Bellflower Ranch. It was an impressive piece of ironwork. At its center, was a flower with drooping petals, painted a faded shade of purple.

Lana hadn't needed her investigative journalist skills to tell her that the bellflower and the Purple Heart insignia were one and the same. Her mother had been in the Air Force. It's why, for most of her life, Lana had spent summers at her grandparents' home. Her mother was often deployed, and Lana had been enrolled in a girls' boarding school for the rest of the months.

Ethan Hunt had also been in the Air Force, but he'd died in combat when Lana was quite young. It was how Lana knew that insignia. It hung on the portrait of her father in her grandparents' den.

Veronica Hunt had thrown herself into her work after her husband's death. Lana's mother had become one of the first female fighter pilots and still continued to fly to this day. The last Lana had heard from Lt. Col. Hunt, she was boarding a Thunderbolt in a location that she was unable to disclose. But at least she'd taken a moment to call her daughter.

Driving through the open gates of the Purple Heart Ranch, Lana saw men atop horses, men bent over tending to livestock, men walking about talking with one another. None of them wore fatigues. But she knew that each of them had served.

It was in the way they walked upright, heads high. It was in the way their shoulders were set. It was in the alertness of their gazes. Soldiers at ease but ever vigilant.

That was how Mac had always seemed to her. Alert and ready, even with his easy smile and relaxed posture. Lana had never felt a moment of fear or uncertainty when she had been with Mac. She'd always felt certain that whatever might come their way, Mac would handle it and make certain she was safe.

Lana brushed the warm rush of feelings aside. She had a job to do. Thoughts of Mac were reserved for the moments before she fell asleep at night. That's when she let all thoughts of him run free in her dreams.

Thoughts of what her life might be like if she'd shown up on her wedding day. Thoughts of lazy Sunday afternoons laying in his arms as she rested her head against his chest as he chuckled and made her laugh. Thoughts of what their children might look like if they'd had their wedding night.

Again, she shook herself. Lana reminded herself that she was awake. In her waking hours, she had work to do. A story to write. Not a fairytale to weave.

Parking her rental car in front of the biggest house on the ranch, Lana climbed out. She ran her hand over her dark slacks and navy blue blouse. The attire was meant to blend in. Letting those around her think she was just a standard-issue military wife and not a reporter hot on a story.

Yup, Lana was going in undercover.

To complete the look, she pulled the pen from her hair and left her notepad in the car. She hated to leave her armory behind, but her mind was sharp enough to record the details of the conversation she intended to have. Though she'd be loathed to use direct quotes without her pen and paper.

Lying wasn't her favorite aspect of her job, but every once in a while, it had to be done. She had tried to come into the situation clean. Lana had called ahead to try and set up an interview. But the person on the other end of the line had declined. The ranch wasn't looking for any publicity, he'd said.

That had set Lana's investigative radar buzzing. Most cults preferred to work in secret. They also isolated their members. A ranch in the middle of nowhere, Montana was pretty isolating.

Though this place was beautiful enough to steal some of her breath. There was actual space enough to stretch out. The greens of the fields were vibrant. The red brick and brown wood of the quaint cabins were inviting. Nothing like the concrete jungle she barely glanced at every day for the last year back in the city.

As she took it all in, Lana felt her shoulders lighten, her chest lift, and her fingers relax. The swinging seat up on the porch looked incredibly inviting. She wondered if she could take a moment to sit there before—

The door of the big house opened, and two men walked out of the house. One was tall and lean. The countenance of a soldier was in his walk. Even though he walked with a metal leg, he moved forward with purpose.

At the soldier's side was an elderly man. The man was smaller in height, but not in the way he carried himself. The older man's honey golden skin spoke of an ancestry of warmer climes. His smile was gentle, welcoming as he regarded Lana. Something in his gaze told her that he could see right into the heart of her.

"Ms. Smith?" asked the soldier.

Lana nodded, absently twisting the band on her left hand. Smith was her cover name. Lame, but also easy to remember. Lana needed to conserve the space in her head for the details she would have to recall and write down later.

"My name's Dylan Banks, and this is Dr. Patel. We're sorry your fiancé couldn't make it on this visit."

Lana flicked the engagement ring up towards her knuckle. "He was recently wounded. He'll be home soon, and I want to have everything ready for him."

Dylan Banks nodded. Though, his shrewd gaze didn't soften as he regarded her.

"I can see the two of you have been separated for a long time?" asked the doctor. The older man's gaze was soft as he regarded Lana.

"I haven't seen him in almost a year." It was the truth. She hadn't spoken to or seen Mac since that last day that she'd climbed out of his bedroom window. She had expected him to come after her, to plead with her to show up to their wedding.

He hadn't. Which hadn't surprised her at the time. He always took a step back when he was trying to win her to his way of thinking. But he'd always step forward again. In the past, he'd never waited more than a day.

"That's hard on a relationship."

Lana could only nod at the older man's words. She tugged the ring down, twisting the diamond until she could feel its point on the fleshy part inside her balled fist.

"You miss him terribly," said Dr. Patel.

It wasn't a question. Because it was the truth. More and more, Lana wasn't able to keep thoughts of Mac confined to just the nights. He had been seeping into her waking thoughts every morning, often at lunch, and a few timed during the workday.

"You should reach out to him soon," said Patel. With another of his gentle smiles, he turned and walked back into the big house, leaving Lana alone with Dylan Banks.

"What branch is your fiancé in?" asked Dylan once they were alone.

"He's an Army Ranger."

Dylan's brows raised. "We have rangers here."

Prickles started over Lana's skin. Not because she thought Mac would be here. The last she'd checked in on his grandparents, they'd said he was still overseas. They couldn't give more details than that, because Mac could never divulge his exact locations. But what if someone from his unit was here on this ranch? She hadn't thought of that.

"What's your fiancé's name?" asked Dylan.

"Mac—elmore. Macklemore. John Macklemore."

"We don't have any soldiers here with that surname," said Dylan. "The unit of Rangers who are here are all in town right now. Planning for a wedding."

Ah! Now they were getting somewhere. "Because in order to stay here, you have to be married?"

"It's a county ordinance. We could fight it and get the rule changed." The soldier before her relaxed his hands, his own gold band gleaming in the afternoon sun. He smiled at something or someone off in the distance. "But the rule has worked out for all of us who've come to live here."

Lana turned to see a group of women and children walking into a field. The women all looked young, close to Lana's age. A group of men approached from the other side of the field. Two of the women went to the men, walking directly into their embraces.

"All of those couples were married here on the ranch?" Lana asked.

A pleased smile spread over Dylan's handsome face. "Each one of them came here to heal from the war and wound up shackled for their troubles."

"How does that work? Do you bring them all together at a dance or something and see who picks whom?"

Dylan's grin flattened. He turned to face her. "No, we're not a dating service or a matchmaking service, Ms. Hunt."

Hunt? Had he just called her Ms. Hunt?

"Or any other salacious thing your magazine might have dreamed up happens on this ranch."

Oh, no. She'd been found out. She'd pushed too hard with that line of questioning.

"This is a place where people come to heal, and they just happen to fall in love. Since it seems you don't believe that, you won't find a story here. I think it best you be on your way."

So much for undercover.

Lana had bitten the dust. But she couldn't go back empty-handed. This was the first real story she'd been given. She just had to find another way in.

CHAPTER SIX

*M*ac pulled up in front of the bridal store in town. He parked the truck in front of the red brick building with white trim. The pink sign on the awning read Nancy's Nuptials.

It was mid-day, and many of the townsfolk were about. A few of the faces Mac knew. He waved to Lieutenant Luke Jackson and his fiancée, Elaine, the town's librarian. Luke was the author of epic military science fiction novels. The retired pilot was working on the next book in the series. The last installment of Luke's books finally had the two main characters coming together for some light romance.

Mac wasn't surprised at the twist in the plot. Not when he watched Luke lean down and kiss the lovely librarian before the two entered their favorite

Mexican restaurant, likely to take advantage of the tacos that were being served up on this sunny Tuesday afternoon.

Mac tugged at his lower lip. He hadn't kissed a woman in almost a year. Not that there hadn't been plenty of chances. There just hadn't been any desire. There was only one woman he wanted to kiss. She was the only woman he'd ever kissed.

When Lana had climbed down from his bedroom window that last night, Mac had been calm. They'd been down this road many times before. Mac would tug Lana in one direction. She would resist and either pull him in a different direction or simply stand still. But eventually, she would give in and go his way.

After waiting until the morning, Mac had gotten a tingling in his chest when she didn't return to his window. The tingling had turned to clenching when he hadn't seen her the next day. The night before the wedding, something inside him had hardened.

For the first time in their relationship, he'd been too tired to chase after her. He'd been too agitated to hold still. He'd been behind all of the progress in their relationship. If she wanted to move forward, she would have to make the move.

She never came.

Instead of going after her with his tail between his legs, Mac had turned his attention to another mission and went back with his Ranger unit. The job had finished a month ago, but Mac still hadn't returned to find the woman he loved.

Yet.

As angry as he'd been at her abandonment, as heartbroken as he'd been at her broken promise to him, it didn't change what was in his heart. If Mac had doubted it then, he knew it now, Lana was it for him. He'd been a goner that first time he'd seen her standing in the bedroom window that first summer.

He'd seen her standing there each summer after for the next ten years. He couldn't help the hope that she would be back there this summer, and they could rekindle what they had.

His friends thought him a fool to go back for yet more punishment. But as the old cliché went, if loving Lana Hunt was wrong, Mac would simply be a fool. Or something like that.

Summer was just a few months away. But now he had another wedding to plan to take his mind off what may or may not be in his future.

Mac opened the doors for Patty and Brenda to climb out of the truck. Brenda wore a grimace as she looked up at the bridal shop like the whole outing was a chore she wanted to pass off to her ranch hand. Mac knew the born rancher would much rather be riding in the midst of her cattle.

Patty, on the other hand, bounced on her toes as though she were a kid standing before the gates of Disney Land. She let go of Mac's hand as soon as her feet hit the ground and made her way to the shop's door.

A wedding bell over the door jingled as they came inside. That was a nice touch, thought Mac. Inside, the shop was a cloud of fluffy white satin, gossamer, and tulle. Mac breathed in the earthy smell of lavender and the spicy scent of orange blossoms and let out a contented sigh. He felt like he was back home at his grandmother's.

Being near Lana wasn't the only reason Mac loved his summers. Spending his days in his grandmother's bridal boutique also held some of his most precious memories. He loved hearing the delighted giggles of the women who came out of the dressing rooms to show off potential gowns. He looked on eagerly as brides' brows drew together in concentration as they poured over pattern books trying to determine the shade that best represented them and their grooms for their wedding colors. His teeth ached as he'd back away from the sweet treats the brides sampled to determine the best recipe for their wedding cakes.

Mac's father had been a bit worried about the boy who loved running in between the gowns and matching colors and patterns. But Sgt. Kenzie had relaxed each afternoon as he watched Mac line up plastic soldiers and gun down the enemies. The sergeant had thrilled as he watched his son chase in vain after that Hunt girl from next door.

"Welcome, welcome."

The proprietress came out from behind the counter, interrupting Mac's reverie.

"My name is Nancy." Nancy reached for Mac's hand and gave a firm shake. "Which one of these is your lucky lady?"

Mac had a flashback to when he'd been planning his wedding. Lana had never wanted to come on these outings, begging off with the excuse that she had to get work done. She'd also used the fact that Mac was much better at "the wedding stuff" than she was. She had a case because whenever she did come along kicking and screaming, she simply deferred to whatever Mac thought was best. With the way clear and no obstructions, Mac had planned an elaborate do... that had never gotten done.

"I'm not getting married," Mac said. "I'm just here for moral support."

"Oh." Nancy turned to Brenda and Patty. "Well, that's just wonderful. Are you both thinking of gowns? Or would one of you prefer a tux?"

Brenda and Patty looked at each other in confusion. Understanding came first to Brenda's green gaze.

"Oh no," said Brenda, holding up her hands. "We're not marrying each other. Not that there's anything wrong with that."

"She's marrying my brother," said Patty. "I'm marrying the love of my life. We're having a dual wedding since we all eloped, and my mother is demanding it."

"How exciting," said Nancy regaining her composure. "Let's get started. Have you chosen your colors?"

"Colors?" asked Brenda.

"I do love pink," said Patty.

"Pink," Brenda cringed. "Aren't we supposed to wear white?"

"How about periwinkle? It's a pastel and could go with pink, for Patty, and green, which is Brenda's best color."

Three pairs of eyes swung around to gape at Mac.

"Then Patty's bouquet could be filled with pink roses. While Brenda could have a more rustic bouquet with green hydrangeas. What do you think?"

The three women gaped silently for a full two minutes.

"I get the feeling you've done this before," said Nancy. She cocked her head and peered down at his hands. "But I don't see a ring?"

Mac thumbed the bare ring finger of his left hand. He offered Nancy a wane smile in response to her flirtation.

"Have you determined your wedding party size?" Nancy was asking.

"No," said Brenda. "I figured it would just be the four of us who are getting married."

"Oh no," Mac piped in. "I'm going to be someone's best man. And then you also need to plan for three more groomsmen since Rusty, Porco, and Spinelli turned up. It looks like you girls will have to come up with four bridesmaids."

Brenda sighed, reminding him so much of Lana. Mac never thought he would meet another girl that didn't gush and obsess over her wedding day. Even now, Brenda was more eager to return to her cattle operation than to spend her afternoon amongst all this frill.

"And now for the reception," said Nancy.

"Oh, that's easy," said Patty.

"Barbecue," both Patty and Brenda said at the same time.

Though Patricia Keaton Hayes loved her sundresses and strappy sandals, the girl could throw down when it came to putting meat on a grill. Mac felt no need to assist with this part of the conversation.

"All right," said Nancy. "I've got most of the details. Let's start picking out dresses."

Watching the women selecting gowns began bringing up too many memories for Mac. What was he thinking volunteering to help with this? One dress, in particular, caught his eye.

It was a simple sheath dress. Most of the decoration was on the lace and beading of the V neck. The thin fabric of the skirt would skim a tall woman's form. The split on the right side would show a trim leg.

It was similar to the one Lana had picked out, though the straps of this dress hung off the shoulders. Mac didn't approve of that design for

Lana. It would take away from the perfection of her collarbone.

He cursed under his breath as his heart skipped a beat at the sudden pang of loss. Mac should've known then that their wedding was doomed. But Lana had insisted on his help, or she would've worn a simple sundress to their wedding.

Mac laid the dress down on the heap Brenda and Patty had collected and turned for the door. He needed some air. "I'll go grab us some grub while you ladies are trying those on."

CHAPTER SEVEN

*T*he green pastures and log-style cabins of the ranches gave way to concrete and brick and mortar buildings as Lana drove her rental into town. The small town reminded her of the one where her grandparents lived and she'd spent her summers. There hadn't been ranches lining the neighborhood streets. But there had been that homey feeling where everyone knew everyone. That feeling where the people walking by looked up and smiled, rather than hung their heads low staring at their phones. That feeling where people crossed the street to say hello instead of going out of their way to avoid any contact.

Lana hadn't been back to her grands' neighborhood since last summer. They talked every

Sunday. But one subject was off-limits. That was the subject of her stymied attempt at marriage. Disappointment always buzzed over the connection.

The buzz was now following her as she walked down the street on a Tuesday afternoon. Lana reached into her pocket and pulled out her cellphone. Looking down at the caller ID, she let out a groan. It wasn't her grandparents calling ahead of their regular time.

"Where are we on the story?"

Reyanna never bothered with greetings. Just as she was ruthless on word count, she was economical with all spoken words.

"I didn't get much from the owner," Lana admitted. "But I have a new angle."

"Good. I need you to move up your timetable. Rucker dropped the ball on another story."

Lana bit her tongue from saying *again*. She had no idea how Nichols and Rucker were still employed at *ChatterZine* if they couldn't keep up with the pace. Their lack of professionalism had steadily provided her footholds up the ladder of success. So, she kept her lips zipped.

"I'm giving you the feature."

Lana unzipped her lips and made a choking sound. She did a little tap dance in the middle of the walkway, unable to contain her delight. Around her, the townsfolk smiled indulgently. One man tipped his cowboy hat. A middle-aged woman gave Lana the thumbs-up sign. They had no idea why she was so delighted, but they seemed happy to take part in her celebration.

This was it.

This was her big break.

"I need the story by Friday night to go in Monday's publication. Can you handle that, Hunt?"

"Yes." Lana found her voice. "Yes, absolutely. I'm on it."

"Don't let me down."

"I won't. I'm on it."

But Lana was talking to a dial tone. Reyanna, having got what she came for, was already off the line. Just as she didn't bother with greetings, the Editor-in-Chief had no use for goodbyes.

A few steps down the street, Lana spotted her destination. Nancy's Nuptials. Dylan had said two brides were in town planning their weddings. When Lana had looked it up, she'd seen that this was the only bridal shop in town.

Wedding bells chimed over her head as Lana entered the small shop. She paused just inside the door. A sea of white lay before her. But not just white. There were linens of cream, ivory, and vanilla. On a table with a milk-white cloth lay an assortment of invitations on stock of polar white, pearl white, and snow white. And then there were the dresses on the racks. Fabrics of porcelain, baby powder, and bone hung just above the floor.

Lana was surprised she remembered so many of the shades of white. She hadn't been paying that much attention when Mac had dragged her into a dress shop a year ago. He'd had to drag her in because she'd been more focused on her deadline than their wedding. She hadn't cared to go dress shopping when she had perfectly good sundresses in her closet. But Mac had insisted.

She'd trailed behind him down the racks of dresses, sneaking notes on her notepad for the story she'd been researching. It wasn't until he'd pulled a dress from a hanger that she'd looked up, and then he'd had her full attention.

If Lana had been the type of girl to dream of her wedding dress, that would have been the dress. She hadn't protested when he turned her toward the dressing room to try it on. He had protested when she'd wanted to step out and show him how perfectly the dress had suited her.

"I'll wait," he'd said.

It was one of her biggest regrets that Mac had never seen how pretty she looked in that dress. It was just a simple sheath dress, but it showed off each of her best assets, making her long limbs appear sexy rather than gangly. Her less than generous breasts got a boost from the intricate beading and lacework.

Lana found a dress that was so similar to the one she'd been meant to wear on her wedding day sitting atop a pile of dresses in the shop.

"That would look lovely on you."

Lana dropped the dress as though it had bitten her. She looked over her shoulder to find a petite woman smiling at her. It was clear that this was the shop's proprietress by the subtle calculation in her gaze.

"When's your big day?"

"Oh," said Lana. "It's... we haven't set a date. It's been a bit of a long engagement. He's deployed."

"Another soldier?" The saleswoman's gaze lost a bit of the shrewdness and added a pinch of amity. "Are you another Purple Heart bride?"

The saleswoman didn't give Lana a chance to answer. She scooped up the dress and took Lana by the arm.

"I've done most of the brides' dresses," the

woman continued as she steered Lana to the back. "Mostly, with only a couple of days' notice. I'm delighted to get a few weeks with Patty and Brenda."

"The Dumasse girls both had a lot of lead time," said a lean brunette, stepping out of the dressing room in a dress that swallowed her whole.

"Ginger Dumasse is that state senator that suggested you and Keaton marry to get around the land regulations?" That came from a curvy redhead who stepped out in a mermaid style dress that made her look like a modern-day Marilyn Monroe.

Lana ignored the dresses and focused on the details she could use for her story. Land regulations? And a politician was in on this?

"The Dumasse girls married soldiers?" Lana asked after the saleswoman left her with the dress and these two sources of information. "From the Purple Heart Ranch?"

"The town's heiress, Honey Dumasse got caught in a compromising position with Private Mark Ortega," chuckled the brunette as she unzipped the gaudy dress.

"Do you mean she got pregnant and had to marry?" asked Lana.

"Nothing like that at all," frowned the brunette.

"The way I heard it," said the redhead, "she lost

her shoe, and Mark found it. Much like Cinderella. Except the ball was a stuffy brunch."

Well, that didn't jive with the story of shotgun weddings and cult-like behavior that Lana was going for. It was far too fairytale-ish. And fairy stories didn't sell magazines.

"I'm Brenda," said the brunette. "And this is Patty."

"Lana."

"Did Nancy say you were marrying a soldier?" asked Patty.

"Yes." Lana held up her left hand. "I'm engaged."

"Congratulations." Both of the women beamed at her.

"Same to you," said Lana, eying their rings. Each woman had two bands on her left ring finger; an engagement ring and a wedding band. So they were already married. "Are you ladies from the Purple Heart Ranch?"

"I own the ranch next door to it," said Brenda, stepping back into the dressing room with a new gown.

"But the magic from there hit both of us," said Patty. Her blue eyes shone with what couldn't be mistaken for love.

Lana needed facts, not feelings. "How so?"

"I was supposed to have a business arrangement with one of the soldiers," said Brenda from inside the changing stall. "I needed money. My soldier needed my land. We even drew up a contract. But then I went and did the girly thing."

"The girly thing?" asked Lana.

Brenda leaned over the top of the stall so that her head was visible. "I looked into his eyes and fell in love. Don't look into their eyes."

Too late, Lana thought, looking down at her own ring. That was what she missed most about Mac. Sitting with him with those clear brown eyes on her as he listened to her with his full attention.

Lana gave herself a shake. It was the middle of the day. Not time to think of Mac. It was time to get the facts for her story. She might be able to do something with the land and regulations angle. But she needed something not so legalese to keep the readers' attention.

Lana turned to Patty, but the redhead was eyeing her in the way of someone trying to remember a dream just as they woke up.

"You look familiar," said Patty. "Have we met?"

Lana was sure she would've remembered the pretty redhead. "I never forget a face. Work habit."

"What do you do?"

Lana decided to keep as close to the truth as possible. "I'm a reporter. I write human interest stories."

Lana thought the woman would push, but Patty's gaze slipped to the dress still in Lana's arms.

"I bet this will look amazing on you," Patty said. "Try it on."

Lana hesitated. The dress was so like the one still hanging in her closet back home. She had no idea why she'd never gotten rid of the dress. Possibly because she still hoped to wear it someday?

She stepped into the changing room and slipped out of her clothes. When she stepped into the dress, it fit like a glove. But she didn't get that tingly all over her skin feeling that she'd gotten with her dress. Still, it was pretty.

"Your new friend?"

Lana tuned into the conversation just beyond the changing room. It sounded like a man had joined Patty and Brenda. The man's voice sounded very familiar.

"Yes, I think she said she was a reporter," said Brenda. "Oh, there she is now."

Lana stepped out of the dressing room. And nearly fell over. There he was.

Well, there his back was. She didn't see his face.

She didn't need to. She'd know those broad shoulders anywhere.

When Mac turned, his brown gaze settled on her. Lana made the mistake of looking directly into his eyes. She felt like she was falling. And then she nearly did fall over as the facts paraded through her mind in quick succession.

Mac was standing there.

In a wedding dress shop.

With two women in wedding dresses beaming up at him.

The girls were both already married.

To a soldier.

There stood one such soldier.

Her soldier.

No, not her soldier anymore. Mac was married to one of those women, and now he was planning his wedding.

At the conclusion of the indisputable facts, Lana lifted the wedding gown, turned, and bolted out of the shop.

CHAPTER EIGHT

*M*ac was having the dream again.

He'd been having this dream since he was a teen, and he'd come to truly understand what marriage meant. In the recurring dream, it was his wedding day. Lana was a vision as she came to him. Dressed in a vibrant vanilla white gown. The design was simple, understated, like the woman who didn't like to draw much attention to herself. Lana had always preferred to sit quietly in the background, observing while she recorded the details.

However, an important detail of this vision was wrong. There was no slit in this dress to show off her slender calves. The straps slid off her shoulders, detracting from the heart shape of her collarbone. It was a feature Mac knew all too well as he'd spent countless afternoons kissing the skin there.

Even with those imperfections, Mac couldn't help himself. He reached for the vision, knowing that the moment her fingers met his palm, it would start the first moment of their forever.

She was so close. He could smell the earthy scent of her morning coffee. He could feel the warmth of her startled breath. He could see the navy flecks in her blue eyes.

But the vision didn't reach for him. Mac's dream woman balled her hand in the fabric of her gown. She lifted the hem of the dress. Then she turned and ran.

That's how he knew he was awake.

Lana had slipped out the window when she'd run from their wedding. At least this time, she dashed away from him in a wedding dress. As things went, he could at least call this run through an improvement.

"What just happened?" said Brenda.

"OMG, she said her name was Lana," said Patty. "That was your fiancée's name, wasn't it?"

"Whoever she is, she needs to pay for that dress," said Nancy.

Mac didn't answer any of them. He truly wasn't

dreaming. It really was Lana. And she was getting away.

Not this time. Mac set off after her.

Lana had always been a fast runner. Mac knew that as he'd chased her more times than he could remember when they were kids. He'd aimed to best her in races when they were adolescents. He could just barely outpace her as a teen. By the time they were adults, he'd kept up a daily running habit to make sure he could always stay one step ahead of her.

She'd had a head start after he'd been struck dumb at seeing her in the bridal shop. She was dashing through lunchtime traffic in the stolen gown. Cars stopped as drivers watched stunned as a bride ran through Main Street.

Lana looked over her shoulder once to see Mac gaining. He would overtake her in a matter of strides, and she had to know it. She feinted right and took a left. Mac wasn't fooled. He kept his eyes on the prize.

She made a mad dash up steps and darted into the first building on her right. Mac followed, certain she had to have missed the steeple at the top of the building she was now taking refuge inside. By the time Mac entered the church, he saw Lana come to a screeching halt in front of Pastor Vance. The young Pastor looked from the out of breath bride to Mac, who wasn't breathing hard at all.

"Do you two need anything from me?" asked the pastor.

"No," panted Lana, taking a step back.

"Not yet," said Mac, taking a step forward.

Lana whirled on Mac. Her face went through three emotions in the span of one second. Anger. Sorrow. Hurt.

Were those tears in her eyes? That brought Mac up short. It was rare for Lana to cry.

Without a second's hesitation, Mac reached for her. He enfolded her into his arms. She came without protest, but not without a sound.

Lana sniffled as her head came to rest on his chest. She took in a shaky breath and let out a sob. Mac felt his heart breaking and racing at the same time.

He pulled her closer. Held her tighter. Tucked the top of her head under his chin and rested his lips against the top of her head. It had been nearly a year, but she still fit into him.

She always had. Since they were kids and they'd sat next to each other, she'd always fit. Whether they were sitting side by side and their shoulders leaned into one another. Or when they'd gotten older, and she'd sat on his lap as he'd kissed her.

Their limbs had always snapped into place. Their breaths had matched. Their heartbeats had synched.

Mac felt Lana's heart racing against his chest. All too soon, it slowed, coming to beat in time with his.

All was right with the world. This was exactly how things should be. Lana in his arms, her heart in time with his.

He had no idea what had brought her here. No idea what had made her cry. He needed to find out and put a stop to whatever or whoever it was.

Mac pulled her away. Slightly. Whatever her answer to his next question, he had no intention of letting her go.

"What are you doing here?" he asked.

Lana glared up at him. Her eyes flashed. As though in an accusation.

That couldn't be right. He'd never wronged this woman. He'd done everything in his power to please and acquiesce her since the first day he'd seen her.

"Let me go," Lana said.

Nope. Not happening. Not ever again.

"I'm sure you have to get back to your fiancée," she said.

His fiancée? Mac's fiancée was in his arms. In a wedding dress.

Why was she in a wedding dress?

Just as soon as he thought of the question, he realized the answer didn't matter. It didn't matter if she was seeing someone else. It didn't matter if she had said yes to another man.

Lana was his. Always had been. Always would be.

Mac took her hands in his. That's when he felt it. He needed to be sure, so he looked down. And there it was.

"You're still wearing my ring," he said.

With her right hand, Lana tugged at the ring on her fourth finger. With effort, she got the band off. They both stared at her bare finger for a moment, both of their chests heaving as though the act of taking off the ring had knocked the wind out of the two of them.

Lana looked up at him. The same anger, sorrow, and hurt still there in her gaze. She lifted her hand and threw the engagement ring at his chest.

Mac caught the band before it could clatter to the floor. His eyes remained glued to the pale flesh on Lana's finger that the band had revealed.

He knew Lana tanned easily. For years, they

would end the summers with her bikini line still visible. Now, it was her ring line that was visible.

Which meant that all through the last fall and winter months that they'd been apart, Lana had not taken his band off her hand.

CHAPTER NINE

*L*ana felt as though she was standing naked in the halls of the church without the ring.

Fitting as she was standing near an altar, in a stolen wedding dress, with the man she'd jilted nearly a year ago. Not only had he taken her ring, but he'd also held her—something Lana hadn't realized she'd needed so desperately. And now he'd let her go.

No ring. No hug. No Mac.

Mac had given her his word that he'd love no one but her for the rest of his life. Yet now he had a new fiancée. No—a bride.

Both Brenda and Patty had said that they were already married, and they were only now planning their wedding. Which one belonged to Mac? Lana had no idea which one. She didn't know Mac's type. Was it the lean, brunette-haired Brenda? Or the curvy, redheaded Patty?

For as long as Lana had known him, Mac had only had eyes for her. But neither woman was anything like her. Patty looked as though she'd stepped out of a fifty's pinup poster. Where Brenda looked as though she could hogtie a bull.

Either pairing would make for a good angle to her story. Only Lana didn't care about the story any longer. She just needed to get out of here. But she didn't want to leave without that ring.

Setting her chin, she lifted her gaze and made a miscalculation. Lana looked up and gazed directly into Mac's eyes. She wanted to fold herself back into him. She wanted to listen to his heartbeat. She wanted to hear his words, his laugh. She wanted to look into those laughing eyes that always urged her not to take herself so seriously.

She'd been so serious for more than half a year. She couldn't remember the last time she'd laughed. Either she was hunched over a desk writing. Or she was crying.

"You have a fiancée?" she said.

Mac sighed. A deep, heavy sigh that seemed to

arise from somewhere deep inside him. The sigh sounded part relief, part resignation.

"Yeah," Mac said. "I have a fiancée."

She'd known it to be true. Hearing the words come from his lips, she felt her heart splintering into a thousand tiny shards. The pieces pricked at her eyelids, and tears sprung anew. "You should get back to her."

"You're right," Mac agreed.

He reached for her again. Lana's brain didn't even contemplate resisting. She came to him, resting her head on his shoulder and nuzzling into his neck.

Mac's lips trailed down the side of her face. It had been so long since she'd been held. So long since she'd been touched.

Lana tilted her head up and met Mac's lips. It was like they'd never parted. Mac's mouth claimed hers.

When they were together, Mac happily let Lana dictate where they would eat, what movie they would see, how they would plan the weekend. But in two things, he tugged the reins away from her and did not give her leave.

The first was their wedding planning.

The second was in kissing.

Mac was a master at kissing. Which had always

puzzled Lana as he swore he'd never kissed anyone but her. She hadn't given in to his kisses until they were eighteen. But even that first kiss had been one for the memory books.

Every kiss after that had been just as perfect. And now, as he kissed her after long months apart, it was the best one yet.

Their kiss wasn't hesitant. It wasn't tentative. It was exacting. Certain. Sure.

It was a meeting of two like minds picking up on an idea that they'd left the night before. His hands splayed across her bareback like he owned her. He slanted his mouth over hers, fitting them together like he was still a part of her.

But he wasn't.

He had turned to someone else.

The thought was a gong in her mind. The ringing of that truth made Lana pull away from him.

Mac let her mouth go, but he didn't let her out of his embrace. That was fine. Lana still needed to be close to him for what she had to do.

She took a deep, heaving breath. Then she slapped Mac across the cheek. Mac's face turned. Though Lana suspected it was more from surprise than the force of impact.

"How dare you kiss me when your fiancée is just a block away."

Mac rubbed at his chin. He opened his mouth wide, rotating his jaw left and right.

"I thought you were a better man than this, Mac Kenzie."

Mac shut his mouth, letting his hand fall to his side. With his hand gone, Lana saw that she'd left a mark. His skin was red from where her palm had met his face.

He peered down at her, as though trying to see her clearly. As the red began to recede from his face, his smile spread. "You think I'm marrying Brenda or Patty?"

Lana flicked her thumb at her fourth finger, only to remember that the engagement ring was gone.

Mac didn't miss the movement. He pulled the ring from his pocket, turning it over in the sunlight from the window. Lana looked away so that he wouldn't see the yearning in her eyes for the band.

"Brenda and Patty are already married," he said. "I was helping with their wedding planning since I've already done it before."

Lana knew that last statement was a dig on her. She ignored it and focused on his earlier statement. "Which one of them is your wife?"

"Neither," said Mac. "Bigamy isn't legal in Montana. Even if it were, I'm sure Grizz and Keaton would object to me nosing my way into their marriages."

"Grizz and Keaton got married?"

Mac nodded, twirling the engagement ring between his knuckles.

"Before you?"

Mac chuckled at that before nodding. "After all their poking at me, and they go and get hitched before I do."

Lana chewed at the inside of her mouth. She remembered his friends. Griffin Hayes and Anthony Keaton. Then there was the whole leaving Mac at the altar bit. She knew she wasn't their favorite person.

But that wasn't important right now.

"You're not married?" Lana asked.

"I never stopped being engaged," he said. "But I plan on getting married. Very soon."

His words sounded like a threat. A threat aimed at her.

"First," he said, taking her hand and tugging her to the door, "Let's get you out of that dress before the sheriff comes after you."

CHAPTER TEN

"There's only this exit, right?" Mac asked Nancy as he stood at the entryway into the changing rooms. The bridal shop didn't have any men's clothes, so there was no reason for him to be back there while Lana changed out of the wedding dress and back into her regular clothes.

"No," said Nancy as she leaned forward against the counter with interest. "This is a one-lane store."

"Good."

Mac crossed his arms and watched the swing door. He could hear muffled shuffles as Lana went about the change. He couldn't help but note that she herself had changed.

It had been nearly a year since he'd last seen her.

Now there were bags under her eyes. The bags had been there before when they were together. Lana had never been the best sleeper. She was a night owl and frequently stayed up late reading, researching, outlining the path she wanted her career to take.

She'd often climbed into Mac's bedroom window in the summers and sat at his desk to do so. Mac would lie on the bed, flipping through wedding catalogs, trying to determine which flowers would best compliment the color of Lana's eyes and would show her off best during their wedding.

"So, that's your fiancée?" said Patty.

Patty and Brenda had each selected a gown while Mac had chased after Lana. The two women had catalogs in their hands, but neither pretended to look down at them. Their gazes were fixed on Mac standing guard at the doorway.

"Yeah, that's her," he said.

"I thought I recognized her," said Patty. "But I'd only seen pictures since she didn't show at the..."

Patty let the sentence trail off. As her voice trailed, Mac's mind wandered back in the past. Memories of his life with Lana swirled around his vision. Arriving at his grandparent's house after a long school year and waiting for Lana's mom's car to pull up a few days later. Walking down to the creek behind their grands' houses, as he and Lana caught up with what had happened during the school year. They were both only children who'd moved around a lot because of their parents' work in the armed forces. Summer was the thing that always remained the same for them.

Even when Mac had gone into the service, he'd finagled his leave to be sometime in the summer months, just so that he could keep their tradition and see her. Even when she'd gotten her first reporting job, she still came back to visit her grandparents and climbed into his bedroom window each summer.

The one and only time she hadn't shown was the day of their wedding.

That hurt had been gut deep. But it hadn't lasted long. By winter, Mac had brushed his shoulders off, knowing that summer was coming. After spring passed, he knew that Lana would come back to him. They always came back to one another.

A hand came down on his shoulder. Mac looked over to find Brenda's serious face. "You okay, Mac?"

Mac nodded, turning his gaze back to the dressing room entrance. "Yeah, I'm good."

He took out the ring that was in his pocket. He still remembered the day when he'd purchased it.

Lana was not really one for jewelry. She knew where all of her favorite pens were. But if he looked in her jewelry box, he'd find mismatched earrings, bracelets with broken clasps, and hair barrettes that were still in their wrapper.

But she hadn't lost the engagement ring. She had never taken it off.

"She told you she was a reporter?" Mac asked.

"Yeah," said Patty. "She was asking questions about the ranch."

Mac knew exactly what Lana was doing here. Dylan had mentioned that a magazine wanted to do a story on the ranch, and he'd refused. Apparently, the magazine was prone to sensationalizing the facts for dramatic effect. No one that lived on the Purple Heart Ranch wanted that kind of attention for their families or the soldiers they served.

And then Lana turned up.

Mac was sure she had a notepad in her back pocket and a pen somewhere in her hair. She was here for the story. It always came back to the story and her career.

The door to the changing rooms opened, and Lana stepped out.

"Why don't you two go talk," said Brenda. "We'll grab a bite and have Keaton come pick us up."

Mac barely registered the girls leaving. Nancy disappeared in the back. Mac and Lana were left on the showroom of a bridal shop surrounded by all things matrimonial.

Mac took a step toward her.

Lana took a deep breath but didn't move beyond his reach.

Mac lifted a hand to her hair. The locks curled around his fingers as though they remembered him.

"What are you doing?" Lana asked.

"Looking for a pen?"

She frowned up at him. Her lips parting as though she were going to ask a question. But her lids hooded as his fingers ran all the way down her scalp to end at her neck.

He had her in his hold. He could do with her whatever he wanted. More importantly, he knew that, at this moment, she would let him.

With his left hand, Mac reached farther down. His hand ran along her spine. Over the belt of her jeans and just a little further. There he found it.

"You didn't come here for me," he asked. "Did you?"

He tugged the notepad from her jean pocket and held it up. On the pad, he saw her neat print organized in sections.

"You think this is a cult?"

"Give me that." Lana reached for the pad.

Mac held it out of her way. "You're contorting what's really going on there."

"They're marrying for convenience. For a house or land or money. Which is what marriage is truly about. It's an exchange. It proves that marriage is antiquated and unnecessary in a day where a woman can make her own way in the world."

Mac studied the woman he'd been in love with for nearly his entire life. Her features were slightly contorted, as though she wore a mask. But he saw deeper. "You no longer believe that people marry each other because they're in love?"

"I believe in love."

They stared at one another. The mask she was wearing was slipping. With an inhale, she fixed her features and stiffened her upper lip.

"Anyway," she went on, "it doesn't matter. None of them will talk to me now that they know I've lied to them. I needed this story. It was going to get me a promotion."

Lana rubbed at her left ring finger. Then she balled her hand into a fist when she found the space empty. They both looked down at her bare finger.

Lana frowned as though something was wrong.

Mac couldn't help but feel the same way. Whenever he imagined her over the past year, it had always been with his ring still on her finger. The reality of this situation needed to be fixed.

Mac took another step to her, closing the distance between them. Then he went down on his knee, holding up the ring between them.

Lana tried to straighten her fingers, but they shook as they hung at her sides. She watched Mac, her brown gaze unblinking. Her chest still as if she were holding her breath. Was that hope or fear in her eyes? Probably a bit of both.

"What are you doing?" she finally managed.

"I have a proposal."

Lana's nostrils flared as though she smelled something delicious in the air that she desperately wanted. Her fingers flexed at her sides, balling and unballing as though she wanted to grab for the ring pinched between his thumb and index finger.

"You're going to help me plan Patty and Brenda's wedding," he said.

"Me?"

"You want an in, and there it is."

Still, on his knee, Mac balled Lana's engagement ring in his fist and waited for her answer. He was quite comfortable in this position, having been down on his knees before this woman five other times before. Maybe the sixth time would be a charm. Especially since the promotion at the magazine was something she desperately wanted more than she wanted him.

CHAPTER ELEVEN

*L*ana sank into the cushions of the plush couch. The frills along the sides where she rested her right arm were giving her a headache. It was because of the zigzag pattern of the lace. Her eyes grew weary, tracing the design left, then diagonal, then left again. She much preferred straight lines and fabric made of much sturdier stuff.

"What do you think for the base color?" asked Nancy, the bridal shop owner.

Lana jerked back as another set of patterns was placed in front of her face. The polka dots of pink, checkered squares of cream, and brocades of blues made her temple pulse with agitation. Lana dug her nails into the couch cushions, only to have her fingers tangle in the delicate lace.

Nancy smiled serenely as she turned the pages of the pattern book, as though each slightly different hue deserved its own in-depth discussion. In reality, each page and pattern had had its own discussion. Not that Lana had said a peep for the last five hours.

"We've been looking at these for fifteen minutes, Nancy," said Mac as he flipped through a second pattern book.

Lana looked at the clock. She was startled to see that it had not been five hours. Not even half an hour. They'd been sitting here for only fifteen minutes, and she wanted to tug her eyeballs out.

"That's all?" Nancy smiled over at Mac, batting her false eyelashes.

Strike that. She wanted to tug Nancy's eyeballs out. Instead, Lana contented herself with pulling at the threads of the dainty lace covering the couch.

"It's tough because Patty and Brenda are such different women," Mac said as he flipped yet another page.

Lana flicked her thumb at the underbelly of her ring finger. The movement which usually calmed her nerves did nothing. Her ring finger was still bare.

Mac had her engagement ring in his pocket. She couldn't ask for it back. What would that look like if she did? Asking the man she jilted for the ring back.

She knew she should've given it back to him. That bit of wedding etiquette she knew. But each time she made to take it off, she never made it past her knuckle. The ring had become a part of her. It had made it seem like it wasn't over between the two of them.

But it was. Wasn't it? That's why Mac had taken the ring back and placed it beyond her reach.

"I'm thinking green," he was saying. "A deep, pastoral green. It would represent the ranch for Brenda. But it would go well with Patty's red hair. Don't you think?"

Mac turned to Lana. Lana wasn't exactly sure what they were talking about? What was a base color?

"I think that is a perfect idea," said Nancy, as she beamed at Mac.

Lana scowled at the woman who leaned a little too close to Mac. Mac hadn't asked for Nancy's opinion. He'd asked for Lana's.

Not that Lana had a single opinion of what to do for Brenda and Patty's wedding. She'd had little to do with her own. Mac knew that. This was all for revenge.

"And for the accents?" asked Nancy.

Accents? Were they speaking in foreign tongues now?

"I'm thinking spring tones," said Mac, "since that is the season."

"You really have a knack for this, Mac." Nancy sighed as she rested her chin in her palm and gazed at Mac.

She'd called him Mac. Wasn't it unprofessional to call a client by his first name? No wonder Lana and Mac were the only customers in the store. What bride would bring her groom inside these doors if the help was going to flirt with them?

But Lana supposed Nancy could flirt with Mac. He wasn't engaged. In fact, he was single and had an engagement ring in his pocket. He was fair game.

"It's not a God-given talent," Lana grumbled. "He learned it from his grandmother, who was a wedding planner."

The two looked over at her. Lana may have said the words with a bit too much vehemence. But they were still true.

Mac only smiled. "See that color on her cheeks?" Mac lifted Lana's chin with his index finger. "She turns that color when she gets passionate about something. That's the exact color of blush I had planned for our wedding colors."

Lana turned away from their gazes. Mac let go of her chin, but she still felt his heated gaze on her face.

"Our colors were blush and plum," he continued. "Plum because there's a hint of that color in her eyes. Can you see it?"

Nancy leaned forward, eyes narrowed as she stared at Lana. "Yes," smiled Nancy. "I think I do."

"It was a beautiful setup," said Mac, closing the pattern book. "Too bad you missed it, Lana."

Mac rose from the couch. Lana was surprised that the delicate piece of furniture didn't groan from his misplaced weight. Lana certainly felt unmoored, as though she were a ship at sea who just realized she'd lost her anchor.

Nancy eyed Lana. The woman's raised eyebrow said it all; *you were stupid to let this one go.*

"Are we done here?" asked Lana.

"For now," said Mac. "We'll let you know about the fonts for the invitations tomorrow, Nancy."

A grumble sounded in the quiet shop. It wasn't Lana's stomach. No, the groan had come straight from Lana's lips. She did not want to come back and discuss fonts.

Mac held the door for her as she walked out. The bells above the shop rang, bidding them a good day.

They walked in silence for a stretch. When they

were younger, they would often spend the day in virtual silence. Mac would thumb through either a bridal magazine or a military one. Lana would read the day's news stories and do her research. They'd been content with one another's presence.

Now, Lana was a ball of agitation. Mac took the engagement ring out of his pocket. He tossed it up, catching it one-handed. The grass beside him was tall. If he missed, it would be lost forever.

"Would you be careful?" she hissed after another throw.

Mac shrugged. "Why do you care?"

She wanted to say that the ring was hers. She wanted to tell him how it had been her only comfort this past year. She wanted to tell him it made her feel safe when she couldn't hear his voice or feel his arms around her.

In the end, all she said was. "Will you be careful, *please*?"

Mac looked down at her. Everywhere his brown eyes touched her face, she warmed. At last, he slipped the ring on his pinky finger. The anxiety inside Lana settled.

They walked on in silence. His shoulders were less than an inch from hers. Lana held her breath with each of their steps, waiting to see if his forearm would brush hers. It never did.

"We got some good work done today," he said once they were at her car. "But I'm going to need you to pull your weight tomorrow. We've got to determine place settings and finalize the invitations."

Lana didn't hide her groan. "I don't see why you need me. You and Nancy were doing just fine on your own."

"Yeah." Mac nodded, looking back down the street where the bridal shop was. "I suppose me and Nancy could handle this on our own."

Lana grit her teeth. She'd known that there was a possibility that Mac had moved on. But in her heart of hearts, she had never truly believed it.

"But, I want you." His voice was soft, but his words were firm. "And we made a deal."

"You trust me to keep my word?" Lana couldn't hold his gaze. Instead, she looked down at his pocket, where he held her ring captive.

Mac's hand came out of his pocket. But the ring remained. Lana watched his fingers as he reached his index finger towards her. It came to rest at the crown of her head. The pad of his finger traced a tender line down her temple. When he came near to her lips, Mac pulled his hand away.

"See you tomorrow?" he said.

Lana had to swallow a couple of times before answering. "I'll be there."

His brows drew together as he studied her. A white tooth flashed as he tugged his lower lip into his mouth. Finally, as though his decision was made, he gave her a curt nod. With a quirk of his brow, he shoved his hand back in his pocket, and turned and walked away.

CHAPTER TWELVE

Mac stared out at the stars and watched them twinkle. His mind raced in time to the flashing of the starlight as it glinted off the engagement ring he held up to the moonlight.

The sun would rise in less than an hour. Sleep had eluded him. He'd been the same on the night before his wedding. Mac had spent the entire day assuring their families and friends that Lana would show the next day. Then he'd spent the night convincing himself that Lana would show in the morning.

She loved him. He loved her. That was all they needed.

Except it wasn't.

Mac had woken the morning of his wedding with a sense of foreboding. It was the same sense he got the last night of every summer since he'd been six and had spent his first summer with Lana. Even at that tender age, Mac had known that when the summer was over, that a good thing was about to come to an end.

The morning of his wedding, he'd awakened with an empty feeling in his stomach. His heart pounded as he rose from the bed. He felt tingles from his fingertips down to his toes as he'd dressed. Lana had had her own apartment near her job at the magazine, but she'd planned to stay at her grandparents' the night before the wedding. The light across the way had not once turned on that night.

In the morning, Mac had gone to the church and made the announcement before all of his family and friends that Lana wasn't coming.

He'd known where she was. He hadn't gone to her office to talk to her. Because he'd known that if he'd seen her smiling while bent over her laptop typing away at a story, it would've truly crushed him.

Mac had spent hours of his life watching Lana writing her stories, smiling to herself as she came up with a clever turn of phrase. He'd always felt a part of her world. But at that moment, as both their families and friends tried to console him, Mac had felt entirely and utterly alone.

His stomach was empty this morning. Mac bypassed the full fridge in the Vance kitchen. He took deep breaths to calm his racing heart, to no avail. He rubbed his fingers against his pants, but the vigorous movements did nothing to stop the tingles at his fingertips.

The first ray of sunlight had yet to touch the ranch. Still, the day's work had already begun. Mac heard Brenda giving orders to Angel, her ranch hand. Keaton was already up and cleaning corals alongside Rusty and Porco. Which left Grizz and Spinelli headed off to prepare the feed. Even though it was spring, the pasture's grass wasn't green enough for grazing.

Mac decided to join Grizz and Spinelli but pulled up short as he walked past the wounded bull's pen. The animal still lay with his belly on the ground, his tail low. A look of defeat in his gaze as he eyed the rising bull who had replaced him.

The once-proud creature looked miserable as he lay in his weakened state. Just a few weeks ago, he'd been the king of the ranch, raring to do what he was bred to do and make nice with the lady cows. The bull had been blindsided, and now he was passed over and all but forgotten. The path before him, so clear a short while ago, was now uncertain.

"So, she's back," came a disapproving growl.

Mac had been expecting this ever since Patty and Brenda had learned Lana's true identity. He'd managed to elude his friends the previous night, which wasn't that difficult as they were both newlyweds and preferred to get wrapped up in their wives at the end of each day.

Mac took a deep breath and turned to face Keaton and Grizz. He knew the looks on their faces. It was the same looks they'd worn as they walked with him out of the church on his wedding day. It was the same looks they'd worn after the third time Lana had turned his proposal of marriage down.

"But you're not with her," said Keaton. "So, I assume you told her exactly where she could go?"

"I'm meeting her later today." Mac leaned onto the railing of the bullpen, looking into the glassy gaze of the bull rather than the glares of his friends.

Keaton cursed under his breath. Grizz only stared.

"Don't put yourself through this again, Mackenzie," said Keaton. "You know exactly how it'll end up."

No, he didn't. This time was different. This time she had come to him.

Accidentally.

But she was still here.

"You said the last time was the last time," Keaton pointed out.

"I never said that," said Mac. "You said that."

"Yeah," Keaton agreed. "After she left you at the altar, proving that she didn't want to be married."

Mac held up a finger in protest. "She didn't technically leave me at the altar. She left me at my bedroom window."

Keaton shook his head. He threw up his hands, indicating that he was done. But not before turning to Grizz and jerking his head at Mac. It was the lifelong best friends' version of tapping the other into the fight.

"Mackenzie," said Grizz. "I gotta agree here. This girl has brought you nothing but pain."

"That's not true," said Mac.

It wasn't. Lana was the bright spot of his life. Keaton and Grizz had never understood that. They'd never given her a chance. All they focused on were the times she'd turned his dates down, or his wedding proposals, or their actual wedding.

"She's never going to commit," said Keaton.

"Says the man who had a five-year plan for a marriage," Mac pointed at Keaton. "And the man who never planned to marry at all." Mac pointed at Grizz.

"Yeah," said Keaton. "But Brenda said yes the first time. Then it only took a couple of days for us to fall in love."

That was the difference. Lana had loved Mac. She still loved him. Of that, he was sure. And if he hadn't been, the proof was still in his pocket.

"Lana keeps telling you no or walking away," said Keaton.

"She kept the ring on all this time," said Mac holding up the evidence. Not only had she kept his engagement ring, she'd kept it on her finger, where every man could see.

"You mean that ring that's in your hand?" said Keaton.

"I took it back," said Mac. "I'm not giving it to her until she asks for it."

Grizz crossed his thick biceps over his chest, but the bulges appeared to soften a bit as he relaxed. Some of the tension went out of Keaton's stiff posture. Could it be? Were they coming around?

"Guys," said Mac, "I know you're trying to protect

me. But you gotta understand, it's always going to be her for me."

After another long moment of glaring, Keaton threw up his hands in surrender. Grizz shrugged his shoulders, letting his arms fall away from his chest. It was all the permission Mac was going to get.

"I'm meeting her in an hour," said Mac. "She's agreed to help me plan your wedding."

"Our wedding?" asked Keaton. "Is that the best idea?"

Mac ignored the question. It was the best idea unless Keaton and Grizz wanted to plan their own wedding, Mac and Lana were the planners that they'd get. "Mind if I take off a little early?"

Mac didn't wait for a response. He walked to the barn where Brenda kept the horses. As he prepared one of the mare's saddle, he couldn't help but notice that his fingers began to tingle once more. As he mounted the horse, his heart began to race before the creature even began to trot. He took off toward the Purple Heart Ranch, and his stomach began to grumble.

What if she didn't show?

CHAPTER THIRTEEN

*L*ana tucked the ballpoint pen into her loose bun. Her notepad was stiff in her back pocket. She walked the grounds of the Purple Heart Ranch under the bright rays of the new day, not bothering to step into the shaded areas. She had nothing to hide today.

In the front yard of the big house that she'd been summarily dismissed from the other day was Dylan Banks. The young soldier ran after a group of small children. His prosthetic leg didn't hamper him as the young ones raced around him. A pack of dogs wove between the man and children. The dogs were a ragtag bunch of patchy fur, missing limbs, and prosthetics of their own. All of the fur creatures looked as though they'd known their own war zone. But every one of them grinned wide, tongues lolling as though they each had tasted love.

Dylan caught one kid up in his arms. The child was a young boy with cafe au lait skin and a riot of dark curls. Dylan tossed the giggling child up and caught him in sure hands. The child looked nothing like the man, but Dylan's face shown with abject adoration as the child scampered away from him to rejoin the melee.

The clouds shifted, casting Lana in the shadows. That's when Dylan's gaze lifted. His grin tugged downward as his gaze landed on Lana.

"Ms. Hunt?"

Lana winced at the use of her real name. "Hello again, Sergeant Banks."

"Sergeant Kenzie said to expect you. I suppose he was the Macklemore you were referring to."

The cloud hovered over Lana's head, but she could feel the sweat trickling down her back. "I'm sorry I lied."

Dylan's brows furloughed and then released. "Why did you lie?"

Lana tugged the pen from her hair, flicked the cap off, then put it back on. "When I called and told the truth, you weren't interested in having your story told. And..." She placed the pen back in her bun. "I needed the story."

"We're private people here," said Dylan. "Families. We don't care to have our business splayed on the covers of a glossy magazine."

"We're a digital magazine, so no gloss."

Dylan did not return her cheeky grin.

"These men and women have suffered enough," he continued. "We've all found peace here, community. I guess you could say it is a bit cult-like."

He lifted that brow that had been furrowed. But now, a deep frown marred Lana's brow. Was he insulted or joking? For all of her skills at reading people and determining their stories, she couldn't get a bead on this man.

"Anyway, Mackenzie vouched for you," said Dylan.

A small smile played at Lana's lips. She hadn't heard anyone call Mac that in a long time. Most of his friends pushed his first and last name together, making him seem like he was some highland conqueror. Lana had to give herself, and the mental image of Mac in a kilt, a shake.

"He said you were the type of reporter who would get to the heart of the story."

"Mac said that?" Warmth flooded from her heart.

It reached around to touch her spine, drying up the sweat that had continued trickling down her back. "About me?"

"Why are you surprised?"

Why was she surprised at anything Mac did? No matter how many times she pushed that man away, he always returned to where she'd left him. Whenever she looked up, he was always there waiting for her. Lana thumbed the bare spot on her left hand, feeling a pang.

"I assume he was the fiancée you were referring to?"

Lana nodded.

"Hmmm." Dylan's mouth went slack as he let the sound tumble from his lips.

"Hmmm?" Lana parroted.

"Just, we've heard a lot about you." Dylan scratched at his jaw as he regarded her.

"Mac told you about me?"

"Since he got here, he's never shut up about the girl he was going to marry. He said the ranch would have no effect on him because he'd already found the love of his life."

Yeah, that sounded like Mac. He'd always been so sure of them. Never a doubt in his mind that they would be together for the rest of their lives. The warmth that had been making a journey all throughout Lana came to a halt. The heat still surrounded her heart, but the beads of sweat returned to her back. There were also some droplets forming on her forehead.

Dylan's gaze stayed on her. His brown eyes pinned her to the spot, asking questions Lana wasn't sure of the answers. She was spared from forming a coherent sentence at the sound of horse hooves.

Looking over, she saw Mac riding atop a beautiful horse. Lana saw his wide grin shining from beneath his cowboy hat. She'd seen Mac in full uniform. She'd seen Mac bare-chested in a swimsuit. But Mac Kenzie, on a horse, with a few buttons of his shirt open, sporting a cowboy hat, made her heart skip a beat, and the sweat gather at the center of her palms.

"Hmmm," murmured Dylan once more.

When Lana looked over at Sgt. Banks, he was no longer frowning at her in disapproval. There was a slight smile on his handsome face.

"Anyway," said Dylan. "I envisioned this place as a haven for the wounded. When men and women come back from combat zones, they, unfortunately, leave a piece of themselves behind in those zones.

Aren't you going to write any of this interview down?"

Lana had been too busy watching Mac dismount and tether the horse. It took her another moment to remember that she had a job to do. She snatched the pen from her hair and whipped out the notepad.

"The Purple Heart Ranch is where many soldiers find that healing both in body as well as in their souls."

"But only if they get married?" Lana asked.

"Marriage is not a requirement to come here to heal. It is a requirement if they want to stay. It's a zoning issue, Ms. Hunt. Not a cult ritual."

"If it's a city or state regulation, you could get it changed."

Dylan's grin widened at that. It was a full-on grin. So bright and full of happiness that Lana thought she understood completely why his wife agreed to their arranged marriage.

"We could get it changed," he agreed. "But it has served us well."

It was a beautiful sentiment, it really was. And if she had been a romantic, or was employed by a romance magazine, it would've been the perfect story. Instead, Lana saw the story she had planned unraveling before her eyes. This place was resembling a cult less and less. It was looking more like a community. Much like the one she'd spent her summers in with her grandparents. Much like the one where she'd fallen in love with the boy next door.

Lana watched as Mac walked toward her. Swaggered was more like it. She had always loved watching him move. Especially when his movements brought him closer to her. Truth be told, she didn't mind watching him walk away either. Because she he'd proven that he'd always return to her.

CHAPTER FOURTEEN

*M*ac took his time getting to Lana.

The sun was behind her, enfolding her in its warmth like a lover's caress. He wasn't jealous of the rays. He couldn't be. The way the light danced over her took his breath away.

Lana watched him too. Her lips parted. Her gaze widened slightly. Her nostrils flared. He'd seen that look in her eyes. It had been there the first time she'd noticed that he was more man than boy.

For much of their time together before that instance, Lana's gaze had always been down, eyes darting over words on paper or pictures on a screen. But that summer day, she'd glanced up at seventeen-year-old Mac. Her pen had stopped moving over the pad. He'd seen that flicker of interest in her eyes, the one where a detail or fact had enthralled her.

"You got enough for your story?" Mac asked her.

Lana tilted her head up to meet his gaze. The move allowed the sun's rays to dance along her neck. Her ballpoint pen was held limp in her hand. She bit at her bottom lip. The pen slipped out of her hand, and Mac barely stopped himself for jumping with joy. That flicker of interest had been for him and not whatever angle she was chasing for this story.

"I'll just leave you two," said Dylan. With a knowing grin, the man turned and hurried after a group moving down the lane.

Mac turned his attention back to Lana. She'd picked up her pen and was looking down at her pad now. The flush slowly fading from her cheeks.

"You don't find it strange?" she said.

"What?" Mac asked, coming closer to her. She smelled the same; coffee beans and cream.

"This place." She pointed the point of her pen. "It's just a little too good to be true."

Lana waved the pad and pen around as though to encompass the whole ranch. Mac ignored her reporter's tools and focused on her hair. The midnight tresses caught the sun's rays as her head turned. Mac bit his lip as the darkness lulled him forward, closer to her.

"Maybe the truth is simply a good thing," he said, stealing a step closer to her.

Lana shook her head at him, blue eyes bright against the creamy skin of her cheeks and the dark roast of her hair. Mac was suddenly dying for a strong cup of coffee.

"You always looked at the world with rose-colored glasses," she said.

"I like roses," he said. "It's good to stop and smell them after the ugliness of combat."

He pursed his lips the second after those last few words left his lips. But it was too late. She'd caught his drift.

After Lana had jilted him, Mac had taken on one more mission with the Army Rangers. It had been a difficult one. But he'd needed to have orders, something to follow. Otherwise, he'd have trailed after her.

Mac had never kept many secrets from Lana. However, he always glossed over the particular details of his time in the service. Telling her instead of the scenery of the places he was stationed and the culture of the people he was sent to help. None of the ugliness.

Not because he didn't think she could handle it. He knew she could. Lana was an army brat, like him. Mac just preferred any moment he spent with her to be one of peace or passion.

Lana's gaze lifted to his. She closed the distance between them. She didn't have far to go because, as always, Mac had already closed much of the ground between them. Her hand rested on his cheek. Her warmth transferred to him, flooding his body with memories of holding her, of burying his nose in her hair, of claiming her lips with his own. The wanting of her nearly knocked Mac to his knees.

How had he spent these many months without her? How had he not run after her that day last summer? Why wasn't he kissing her right now?

"Did you get hurt?" Lana asked.

Mac's grin wavered. He took her hand from his cheek, enfolding her fingers with his. "I went in hurt."

Lana's eyelids shuttered. She pressed her lips together and swallowed.

Mac wanted to curse. It had been too long since he'd looked into her eyes. But he couldn't take the words back. They were the truth.

"I didn't want to hurt you, Mac." She shook her

head softly but didn't open her eyes. "I just wasn't ready."

Mac stared down at Lana. As he did so, he felt his heart skipping beats at just the sight of her. He felt his chest fill with air, waiting to sigh a longing exhale as he took her in. At her cheek, his fingers started to curl with want.

Mac snatched his hand away from her face and took a step back.

"We'd been dating for years," he said. "Marriage was the logical next step."

Lana's eyes slammed open and then narrowed on him. "We hadn't been dating for years. You had chased after me for years. We'd only officially started dating two years ago. You asked me to marry you on our second date."

"You knew I'd been in love with you for years," he said.

"*You* fancied yourself in love. *I* was still trying to figure out who I was."

"Fancied? Since when do you say words like fancied?"

"It just happened so fast." Lana shoved the pen behind her ear, but the pad she kept in her hand and waved it at him as though it contained evidence to support her angle. "I said yes to a date. You declared that we were boyfriend and girlfriend by the weekend. Then you were down on your knee proposing the next week. I didn't have time to catch my breath."

"Why would you need to catch your breath?"

"Because I wasn't sure." The pages of her notebook fluttered irritably as she threw up her hands. "You had our story all written out. You barely allowed me to add any details. It was all according to your outline."

Mac rocked back on his heels. "Are you telling me you didn't feel the same way that I did?"

"Yes, I did. Of course, I did." Lana shoved the notepad into her back pocket. "Eventually."

Mac's heart stopped skipping beats. Instead, it raced to keep up with the pacing of this revelation. Lana had always been a cautious girl, wanting to know all the details before committing to anything. That's why he'd planned everything; their courtship, their dates, their wedding.

"You said you knew you loved me from that first day when you were six." When she said it, she sounded exhausted, not delighted.

"No, I said I knew I was going to marry you when I was six."

"I didn't know where I was going to be from one

month to the next, and you were trying to plan my future."

"I was planning *our* future."

"Sure." She crossed her arms over her chest, her fingers squeezing at her forearms. "With peach base colors and plum accents."

"Blush," he corrected. "It complemented your skin tone." Oh, she had gone too far if she was disparaging his wedding planning skills. "You said you didn't care what I chose. You said that you only wanted to have to show up. And you couldn't handle that."

Lana reared back at those words. Her hands dropped to her sides, and her fists balled.

"I'm sorry," he said.

And he was. For more than half his life, Mac had lived to make this girl smile. He'd hung on her every laugh. He'd cherished every touch. Even now, his heart raced, and his chest begged for air, and his hands itched to be filled with her.

"No," she said through gritted teeth. "I'm sorry. I'm sorry that I hurt you. But even more, I'm sorry that my plan for my life interfered with the plan you had for my life."

She turned on her heel so quickly that her pen lost its hold in her hair. It fell to the ground with a silent thunk. She didn't turn to pick it up. Mac doubted if she even noticed it was missing.

He should let her go. He should at least give her a moment to cool off.

Mac bent down to pick up the pen. He rolled the tool in his hands. Then, he couldn't help himself. He ran off after her.

CHAPTER FIFTEEN

*L*ana stormed away from Mac, needing to put distance between herself and him.

Mac had been relentless in their childhood. Knocking on the door to ask her to come out and play. Even if she said she was engrossed in a book, he'd simply lay on the floor until she gave in and came outside.

When they were teens, he asked her to go on a date with him every Friday afternoon. Even when she said she just wanted to be friends.

Once they'd started dating, he waited only a few days before the first marriage proposal. Even though she was still acclimating to the feeling of her first kiss.

The entire time she'd known Mac Kenzie, he'd

pushed and prodded and cajoled until she gave in and did what he wanted. But the problem was that Lana always loved going out and playing with him as a kid. She had the most fun on their dates as a teen. When he'd asked her to spend the rest of her life with him, her heart hadn't skipped a beat. It had settled like it found the perfect spot to set down roots.

However, it was all still a whirlwind. She hadn't been able to catch her breath since she was six years old. Even now, she could hear him behind her as she stormed into the nearest building she came across.

"Mac, stop." Lana whirled around. "Please."

Of course, he kept coming. As though something like her outstretched hand, or the crinkle in her eyes, or her very words would deter him.

"Please."

Wonder of wonders, his steps slowed. He left a foot of space between them. And then, instead of haranguing her, he asked, "Do you want me to leave?"

Just looking at him made Lana's heart rate slow. Her breathing came easier. How was it that he could make her heart race and settle at the same time? How was it that he could leave her breathless and calm her breathing at the same moment? Why was it that she needed both distance and nearness from this man all in the same space?

When she didn't immediately answer him, he took another step toward her.

"Mac," Lana warned, bringing her hands back up. If she stretched her fingers, she'd brush his chest.

"You're upset," he said.

"Because you're making me upset."

"That's not what I want." Mac reached his hand out. Instead of touching her or bringing her close to him, he opened his palm. In his hand was her pen. "Tell me what you want me to do?"

Lana stared at the proffered pen. Her chest rose and sank with short breaths. She took a deep inhale, preparing to tell him. To tell him what? That she wanted him to go away, but kiss her at the same time. That she wanted him to hold her, at the same time that she wanted to punch him in the nose.

She took the pen and shoved it back behind her ear. When she looked up, it was already too late. Mac had closed the distance. His arms were already around her. But he didn't bring her into a tight hold. His hands simply rested on her shoulders.

"Mac," Lana sighed.

"Yes?" His hand cupped her cheek.

Lana felt the cool metal of her engagement ring

on the side of her face. She placed her hand over his, rubbing the ring that was on his pinky. It instantly brought her comfort. She knew what she wanted. She wanted it back.

The ring. She wanted the ring back. But did she want what came attached to the ring?

As though he could read her mind, Mac brought his face closer. Too tired to fight, she waited for the inevitable.

He always did this; he wore her down until she gave in to his demands. When the kiss she knew was coming didn't, she frowned up at him.

"I want to kiss you," Mac said. "Is that something you want?"

Lana bit her lip. She knew that if she gave him an inch, he would take more than a mile. He would take her mouth and all of her reasoning.

"Tell me what you want, Lana, and I will give it to you."

Lana closed her eyes and rubbed her cheek against the ring, searching for the peace it had brought her over the year that she and Mac had been apart. That ring had been her security blanket in the storm her life had become without him there to anchor her. It had been the promise that she'd held on tight to.

She wanted the ring back. Would it hurt to have just a small taste of him too?

Lana lifted her gaze. Her blue eyes cleared when they met the twinkle at the center of his brown gaze. Whatever Mac saw in her gaze gave him the answer to the question he'd posed a second ago. His mouth crashed into hers.

Mac Kenzie did nothing by halves. He went all out. He claimed what he knew had always been his as he deepened the kiss.

Lana could deny it all she wanted, but her heart had always belonged to this man. It always would. No distance. No space. No breath would ever change that.

No matter who had outlined their story. No matter when the details got filled in. This was always how the story of Lana Hunt and Mac Kenzie was meant to go.

Mac pulled her into his embrace. His hand slipped from her cheek and came to her low back, pressing her into him. Lana mourned the loss of the ring's cool touch for only a moment. The fire burning between them was too bright for her to care.

The sound of the ringing didn't immediately pull her attention from Mac's kiss. It was Mac's hand moving into her pocket to grab the phone that did it.

Before he could pull the device out, Lana had come back to her senses.

She frowned at his actions. Mac only shrugged, not an ounce of guilt in his grin. One arm still fit tightly around her.

"It's my editor," Lana said, snatching the phone from him.

"Send it to voice mail," Mac growled.

"No. I need to take this," she insisted, pushing against this chest. "I want you to please give me some space."

Mac gritted his teeth as the ringing continued. Finally, he relented and let her go. However, he didn't go. He simply leaned against the wall and peered down at her. Lana rolled her eyes and stepped out of the building.

As per usual, Reyanna didn't bother with a greeting. "Lana, what's the update?"

"I got access to the ranch. I'm conducting interviews now."

If the Chief saw just how Lana was conducting her research, she might raise an eyebrow.

"But the story is taking a different direction," Lana continued. "These people living on the ranch, they're families. I'm thinking of spinning it as a feel-good story about healing the heart as well as the body."

Dylan Banks' words had sounded corny to her the other day. The words rang different to her ears now. Perhaps because her heart still pounded from a long-overdue kiss.

"Hmmm, no," said Reyanna. "Healing doesn't sell copies. Scandal does. Let's stick with the cult angle."

Lana glanced out in the field at the families picnicking. She spied Dylan Banks bury his nose in a pretty brunette's hair. Two dogs ran around their feet, and a toddler waddled up to them.

"This story is going to get a feature," the Editor in Chief was saying. "That will solidify your career here at *ChatterZine*."

Behind Lana, Mac came back to the entryway. She felt his presence before she turned to him. The corner of his mouth lifted in that knowing gaze, the one that said, You know you want to, and I'll wait patiently until you change your mind. Lana tried to turn away, but she couldn't escape the heat that still burned in his eyes.

"Will that be a problem for you, Hunt?"

"No. No, it won't."

CHAPTER SIXTEEN

The sun slowly sank down below the horizon. The last ray warmed the sweat at the center of Mac's shoulder blades. He put away the last of the tools. But he kept the screwdriver, tucking it into his shirt pocket. As the other guys piled in Keaton's truck to head into town for a cold drink, Mac jumped into the driver's seat of his own car.

Grizz and Keaton avoided his gaze as they had been doing all day. The two men didn't need to voice their disapproval of where Mac was headed. Rusty and Porco, the two men who believed in love, gave him an encouraging nod. While Spinelli, the brains of the bunch, frowned at Mac as though he had no clue what was going on.

When Mac arrived twenty minutes later, he parked in the lot of the town's only motel. The establishment was a quaint one-story, ranch-style layout. It wasn't a chain, but owned and operated by a family. Hopping out of his car, Mac slung a cloth bag over his shoulder. The heavy square contents slapped at the right side of his shoulder blades.

Mac bypassed the front door. He made his way around the back of the establishment. The small Montana town wasn't exactly a tourist destination. There weren't many people staying. So it was easy to spot the window he wanted.

The curtain was parted, and he saw a figure hunched over a laptop inside. Mac pulled out the screwdriver from his shirt pocket and got to work. It took just a few flicks of his wrist to wrest the window open. He heard a slight gasp as the screen gave way. The window's sill was low enough for him to simply raise his leg and step inside.

Mac took a moment to replace the screen and glass, making sure to tighten the screws securely. He didn't want some crazy stranger trying to make their way in here later tonight. Then he strode into the room like he belonged there.

Because he did. Wherever she was, was where he was meant to be.

Lana only stared. Her beautiful eyes wide, but not exactly surprised. Her cheeks were flushed. Her lips parted. Her slender fingers hovered over the middle keys of the keyboard.

When he was close enough, Mac bent down and brushed his lips lightly over Lana's. Just a taste. He didn't press his suit. He knew she was working. He had work of his own to do.

With a smile and a rub of his nose against hers, he took the two strides over to the made bed. Kicking off his boots, he sat himself down, crossed his legs, and took out the sample book from his satchel. He had to nail the fonts for Brenda and Patty's wedding tonight to get the information back to Nancy, so she could start on the invitations.

The massive book opened with a crack and crinkle of paper. After he'd turned a couple of pages, Mac heard the scoot of the desk chair and the clacking of keys resume. He settled back into the pillows of the bed. The puff of air that escaped the soft pillow carried a whiff of Lana's bright scent. Mac made himself even more comfortable, preparing to stay for a long while.

The scratching of pen on pad, the clicking of nails against keyboard, the soft sighs of concentration that escaped her lips were all welcome sounds to his ears. Pretty soon, Mac was lost looking at fonts of serifs and sans serifs, trying to find a happy medium between the block lettering and curly type to fit the two brides. He was so engrossed in looking at fonts that he didn't notice when the tapping of keys stopped.

The mattress dipped. The earthy scent of tart beans with the sweet hint of rich cream filled his nostrils. Warmth invaded his right side. Mac looked over to see that Lana had joined him on the bed.

"Hey," he said.

"Hey," she said.

They simply gazed at each other for a moment. It was as if the last year had melted away, and they were just the two of them sitting in one of their summer bedrooms again. A rightness settled over Mac, a feeling he knew he was going to fight to maintain.

She'd said she needed space. Being in the same room with her, but sitting a few feet apart was the best he could do. It was Lana who had closed the distance this time.

She tugged at her bottom lip with her teeth. Her throat worked as she swallowed down whatever she'd been about to say. Her gaze dipped, but not to his lips. Her eyes rested on his left hand, more specifically on the pinky finger of his left hand.

Mac saw her rubbing the bare fourth finger of her left hand. Her nostrils flared as she continued to eye the engagement ring. She licked at her lips, as though she were thirsty. Her mouth was right there for the taking. She was ripe for the claiming.

"What are you looking at?" Lana asked.

Mac almost told her exactly what he was looking at and exactly what he wanted to do with what he was looking at. But she wasn't looking at his face. Her focus was on the book in his lap.

"I'm trying to choose the perfect font for the wedding invitations."

"Need some help?" Lana scooted back into the headboard of the bed.

Mac's mouth fell open. "Really?"

"It was part of our deal, right? You help me get access to the ranch, and I help you plan the wedding."

That had been the deal, but Mac hadn't expected her to keep her end of the bargain. He was happy that she hadn't left town now that she'd gotten the interview. Happier still that she hadn't kicked him out of the motel room. Hearing that she was willing to help him with this plan, he... Well, he didn't quite know what to think?

"I don't know how much help I'll be," Lana said. "You know I don't have a knack for any of this."

"Well," Mac leaned forward, pushing the sample book cover over until one side of it lay in her lap. "You could approach it like you would a news story."

Lana's brow lifted, the way it did when she was curious about some detail. "I only just met Brenda and Patty. They're very different women. Keaton and Grizz..." Lana grimaced, tucking her legs under herself, which pushed the sample book off her lap. "I never really got close enough to them. I know they don't like me."

"That's not true," said Mac. The sample book fell to the other side of his lap, forgotten. "They just don't know you."

"All they know is that I keep hurting their friend." Lana tugged the pen from her hair and set it on the side table.

"I was your friend first." He brought his finger to her temple and traced the line of small hairs he found there. "You know me better than them. You know me better than anyone."

"You know me better than anyone, too." She

moved closer until their knees bumped. "Are we gonna talk about... it."

"It?" Mac raised a dubious eyebrow at her.

"You know what I mean." Lana dropped her gaze. "Our wedding."

"We didn't have a wedding."

As the sigh escaped her lips, her shoulders deflated. Instead of sinking into herself, she sank into him. Mac had made the first move at every stage of their relationship. But this time, it was Lana who leaned in and brushed his lips.

"I missed you," she said, her voice so soft the only way he knew she'd said anything was the movement of her lips against his and the brush of her breath on his tongue.

"I know," he said.

Lana pulled back, indignation evident on her beautiful face. She punched his shoulder, but she grinned as she did it.

Mac caught her hand in his. Absentmindedly, he rubbed his thumb over her knuckles. He watched as her throat worked when his thumb came to her left ring finger and rubbed the bare skin there. The moment was ripe to offer her the ring again.

Instead of pulling her into his arms and claiming

what he knew in his heart was his, Mac let go of
Lana's hand. He pulled the sample book back
between them. Lana scooted closer, snuggling into
his shoulder as they looked at the fonts.

CHAPTER SEVENTEEN

*W*armth spread across Lana's shoulder blades. She turned with a smile on her face, preparing to greet the source. Instead of warm, virile man, she met with the rays of the morning's sunlight.

Mac was gone. He'd stayed until late in the night. They'd chosen a font for the upcoming double wedding. Then moved onto writing the words for the invitations that would be printed in the chosen font. From what Lana knew of Keaton, who liked to plan, and Grizz, who liked to brood, Lana thought she'd helped make a good decision with the word choice. There were the details—date, time, place—written in bold. The dress code stated come-as-you-are, as though urging guests to think deeply about their attire.

After the invitations, Lana had assumed the rest of the night would be devoted to catch-up-kisses. But Mac had pulled a long list of things to do for the upcoming nuptials. Lana hadn't known that so much had gone into planning a wedding, being as Mac had taken care of every detail of theirs. They'd gotten another five items crossed off the list.

And then came the kisses. Though the make-out session hadn't been initiated by Mac. He'd stood, as though preparing to leave, and that's when she'd reached up and brought his head down to hers.

Mac had always been the initiator in their relationship. Not this night. He hadn't made any moves on her since he'd cornered her in the barn and asked her what she wanted. Had it been a year ago, he would've already made the plans and kept at her until she'd agreed.

Last night, he'd let Lana control the kisses. He'd let Lana determine how tightly she'd wanted to be embraced. He'd let Lana determine when it was time to stop. Although she couldn't remember why she had. She had no idea how she had survived the last two hundred eighty-five days without beginning and ending every day with her lips pressed against Mac's.

He'd left shortly before midnight. Unlike his grand entrance, he'd used the door upon his exit, wanting to make sure the window was secure as she slept. Lana had hated watching him go. But he'd promised to pick her up tomorrow to have dinner at the ranch.

The clock on the bedside table told her she still had half the day before he arrived. Should she call him...?

No. He said he'd be working on the base training camp he and his friends were building. Maybe she could stop by and...?

No. If there was one thing about Mac, he'd never interfered with her career. He'd never stopped by the office unannounced. Nor had he put up much of a fuss when she'd stayed late. The only time he'd put his foot down was for their wedding weekend when Lana had chosen to chase a cat story over him.

Lana stared at the computer screen. She'd finished the first draft of the ranch exposé. From her research on cults, Lana had gathered that many leaders had a number of personality characteristics in common. Cult leaders were often charismatic narcissists who were hierarchal, unpredictable, and engaged in devious carnal activities with their members.

Not a single one of those characteristics described the Purple Heart Ranch's leader, Dylan Banks. The man, who Lana had learned came from great wealth, was incredibly down to earth, personable, kind to animals, and completely head-over-heels for his wife. The only thing he had remotely in common with the Charles Mansons and Jim Joneses of the world was his desire to be separate from the outside world. And, so, the article focused on the exclusivity of the rehabilitation ranch. It highlighted the speed at which the residents got married. It pointed to the ranch's psychologist, who also was the church pastor that had married every single man and woman in residence.

In short, it was sparse on facts, loose with substance, and the worst thing Lana had ever written.

She opened a new document on *ChatterZine*'s shared cloud drive and began again. The cursor blinked at the word *cult,* and Lana couldn't figure out what to put after it.

After four taps of the delete button, Lana began again. She started with the women she'd met on the ranch. The veterinarian who was the first bride, Maggie Banks, and her animal rescue efforts. Then there was Eva Demonti, who was finishing up a social worker degree that she planned to put to use with the migrant and immigrant workers in the state. Sarai Cannon was a beauty blogger who's work, which focused on inner beauty and self-love at all shapes, sizes, and colors had really impressed Lana. Those three were just the beginning.

While the men were having their bodies healed, it was the women of this ranch that were changing the world around them. Lana's fingers flew across the keyboard. Once she reached the end, she scrolled back to the top having determined the perfect title; *The Purple Rush Brides*.

She knew in her heart that once Reyanna read the new story, the editor-in-chief would change her mind. It was going to make readers feel good at a time when there was so much strife in the world. Lana was still editing and playing with word choice when there was a knock on her door. She glanced at the time and couldn't believe how much had passed.

"Just a minute," she called as she flipped open her suitcase.

"That means you're not dressed because you were still working," came the deep voice on the other side of the door.

Lana sniffed under her armpits. Coming away

with a wrinkled nose, she dashed into the bathroom. "What? I can't hear you."

"That means that not only am I right, but you haven't showered either."

Oh, that man.

"Which is why I told you to be ready an hour before you needed to be."

Lana made a face, even though he couldn't see her. She was not normally late. Except when it came to their dates.

"You're making a face at me, aren't you?" Mac laughed. "I'll be outside waiting for you."

Lana hopped into the shower, throwing water and soap all over herself. She did her makeup as she toweled off. Then slipped into a sundress. She was ready in twenty minutes.

When she stepped out, Mac grinned at her. He stood in a fresh pair of jeans and a crisp collared shirt. The man was truly beautiful. He leaned patiently against the truck like he would've waited forever.

He held his hand out to her. There was not a flicker of concern on his face like he didn't doubt she would come to him. It reminded her of the first time he'd proposed. She'd said no. He'd frowned, but a second later, it was as though she hadn't turned him down, and they continued on with their date.

Mac never doubted that she would be his friend, his girlfriend, his wife. Anytime she'd said no or turned him down, he'd bounced back a second later. Not exactly more determined. He always had the same amount of determination. It was as though he'd always known she would say yes.

Eventually.

Because she always did say yes to him. He'd never really poked or prodded her. He'd take her rejection as his due, and then later try again.

Lana took his hand now. He brought her fingers to his mouth and kissed her knuckles. Then he leaned in and kissed her lips. Just a light brush of skin to skin. He didn't press his claim. He didn't need to. Like always, the eventual moment had come.

She was his. She had always been his. She would always be his.

They drove across the town, as Mac told her about his day. Each time he tried to turn the conversation to her, she turned it back on him. She loved his enthusiasm for the camp they were building and wanted to know all about it. She wondered if she could pitch an angle for the story for *ChatterZine*?

All too quickly, they pulled into Vance Ranch, where Mac was staying. Unlike the Purple Heart Ranch, there were cattle dotting the skyline and hardly any people mulling about. She did see a few familiar faces coming down from the porch of the big house.

With her red hair flying behind her, Patty rushed to Lana and swallowed her up in a hug. "It's so good to see you again, Lana."

Behind Patty, Brenda tipped her cowboy hat. "Welcome to Vance Ranch."

"Thank you for having me," said Lana.

"No, thank you for helping Mac out with the wedding plans," said Patty. "He said you helped word the invitations. It's so good to have a writer in the family."

A deep male voice cleared his throat. Keaton offered Lana a tight grin that did not meet his eyes. "So, when are you leaving, Lana?"

Brenda punched her husband in the shoulder. Patty shot her brother a murderous gaze. Mac rested his hand at Lana's lower back. Lana sank into the warmth he provided her.

In truth, it was a fair question. The story she'd been sent to write was pretty much done. She'd have to get back to work. But the thought of leaving Mac did not sit with her.

"I'm not sure," she said finally. "My work here is done, but I don't have a new assignment yet, so…"

Lana let the sentence trail as she chanced a glance at Mac. He didn't meet her gaze. His eyes were instead focused down on her hand. Belatedly, Lana noted she was rubbing the bare flesh of her left ring finger.

"Mac said you were writing a piece about a cult?" said Grizz.

"That's the angle the magazine wanted," Lana admitted. "I found a different angle."

"What angle is that?" asked Patty.

"Instead of focusing on the men, I decided to focus on the women and how they are changing this community. It's a piece about how marriage isn't about convenience, it's about coming together to make you and the world around you stronger."

"That sounds amazing," said Patty. "I can't wait to read it."

The two pairs turned and started up the steps that would lead into the big house. But Lana held back. Mac turned to look at her.

"Hey, Mac?"

"Yeah, Lana."

Lana scratched at the agitated skin on her ring finger. "Can I ask you something?"

"What?"

"Can I have my ring back?"

Mac cocked his head as he regarded her. He reached down into his pocket without looking. "This ring?"

A sense of relief washed over Lana as she saw the gold band. The diamond caught the setting sun and twinkled as if giving her a warm welcome after being apart for long.

"What do you want it for?" Mac asked.

"It's just..." Lana took a deep breath and let it out slowly. "I've been feeling kinda lost without it. And I want it back with me for the rest of my life. Because I never actually took it off. I never intended to. These last couple of days, I realize just how much I need the comfort it brings me. I love that ring. So, can I have it back? Please?"

Mac's face was impassive as he regarded her. Lana was an ace reporter. She knew how to ask open-ended questions to get her subjects to divulge their knowledge. But in this case, Lana only wanted one answer. And she wasn't sure how or if she'd get the answer she craved.

Before Lana could craft a new set of interrogative

questions, Mac slipped the ring off his finger and held it out to her.

Lana lifted her left hand, palm out, waiting for him to drop it into her waiting palm. Mac held up the ring, the band hovering just over her fourth finger. Mac aimed the ring, but before it slid over her nail, Lana stopped him.

"Hey, Mac?"

He lifted his gaze. "Yeah, Lana?"

"Do you think... I mean, would you mind..."

"Yeah?"

"Can I still marry you?"

Mac grinned, slipping the ring on her finger. Lana felt that sense of grounding again. She felt like part of her had been missing, not just for a couple of days, for nearly a year.

"Yes, Lana. Yes, you can marry me."

CHAPTER EIGHTEEN

"Don't you think you should give this some thought?"

Mac didn't need to ask Keaton what he was referring to. The man had never liked Lana. Neither him nor Grizz. Probably had to do with the many times Mac had come to his friends moaning about her latest rejection.

"What thought?" said Mac. "This was always the plan."

Truthfully, there had been some thought. Mac had taken a different tactic this time in his pursuit of Lana. He'd waited and let her come to him. Instead of years, instead of months, it had taken only days to get her back. And this time, she'd proposed to him.

He'd barely eaten last night at dinner because

153

his grin had been so huge. His hands had also been more interested in twining with Lana's than handling his fork. His nose had preferred her robust coffee and cream scent, and his eyes could care less for the perfectly seasoned steak and wilting veggies that had also been burned at the edges. Instead of partaking in the meal, he'd been consumed with Lana, his woman, and once again, his fiancée. Soon, she'd be his wife.

"Gotta agree with Keaton," said Grizz. "You're rushing into this."

Mac kicked a foot up against the railing as he looked on at his two friends in utter disbelief. "Says the two men who married their wives within a week. How am I doing anything different from what you two did?"

"You two just have a history," said Keaton, giving his cowboy hat a flick up and off his forehead.

"It's different this time," said Mac. "You have to see that. She came to me. She proposed to me."

Keaton and Grizz shared a look. Mac was getting tired of those shared looks. The two were best friends and had years of history behind them before they'd met Mac. Mac had never begrudged them their friendship and their silently loud looks. He and Lana had their own inside jokes and telling gazes.

"What about the details?" said Keaton. "Have you talked about where you'll live?"

No, they hadn't. But Mac knew better than to ask Lana to give up that job. It was his only competition for her attention. It had come between them the first time. Now she was likely getting a promotion. Would she leave it? Or would she expect him to go back with her?

Mac looked around at the camp. They had sectioned off the training area. Now that the others had arrived, they were making real progress, and the physical fitness obstacles were nearly all erected. They were going to deliver some serious pain to their first set of recruits, and Mac couldn't wait.

Where would Lana fit into this? A life with Lana had been his dream since he was six. This camp had been his dream since Basic Training. Could he give up one dream for another?

"We haven't talked about that," Mac admitted to his friends. "But, we will."

"You think maybe you should have that chat before walking down the aisle this weekend?" said Grizz.

After the congratulations at dinner last night, Mac and Lana had settled on a weekend wedding. The women had cheered. Keaton and Grizz had shared another one of their deafening glances. Rusty, who had unsigned divorce papers in his bag, looked out the window. Spinelli, a confirmed bachelor who planned to never marry, frowned in incomprehension. Only Porco, who was an admitted ladies' man offered up congratulations.

The back door to the big house had opened, and Brenda's brother had come in with two foil-covered dishes, saving the group's arteries from a steak only dinner. No sooner than he put down the buttery veggies did he learn about the good news. Pastor Vance had joked that he could marry them that night.

Mac wouldn't hear of it. He had to have at least a few items in place for his wedding day. He'd dreamed about this moment all his life. And so they'd settled on the weekend.

There was a gazebo on the Purple Heart Ranch. He could have that place decorated in their wedding colors in a few hours. He knew the flower shop needed a few days to order matching flowers. He'd already put in a call with the bridal shop about place settings that were available within that time period.

And then what?

Don't you think you should give this some thought?

Mac had thought about the wedding day. Had he

really thought past that? Had he thought about the future that came after the marriage? The fact of the matter was that he didn't see a future without Lana in it. What exactly did that future with Lana look like?

"I'll catch you guys later," Mac said as he climbed into his truck.

His day at the camp wasn't done, but after the hours he'd put in before Rusty, Spinelli, and Porco finally made it, Mac knew he was due a little slack. Especially if he was getting married this weekend.

After driving across town, Mac parked in front of Lana's motel. He started for the front door, but his path took him to Lana's window. When he came to it, he saw that she had left it open for him to climb through.

Peering inside, he saw her sitting at the small desk, her laptop open. Her left hand was raised. Her thumb ran back and forth over the band on her ring finger. She rolled her neck, letting out a sigh that resonated with deep contentment. As her head moved to the side, Mac caught a glimpse of her computer screen. Instead of a page of words, she was looking at a wedding site.

Mac tripped as he stepped over the window, but caught himself before he hit the ground.

"Hey." She grinned up at him.

"Hey," he said straightening.

"Come see." She waved him toward her screen. "I know you've got the decorations for the gazebo covered, but I was thinking about our reception and—"

"You were thinking about our reception?" he parroted.

"Yeah, and I came across this site as I was looking at centerpieces and—"

"You were looking at centerpieces?"

"Why are you repeating everything I say?"

"Who are you, and what have you done with the woman I love?"

Lana rose with a laugh. She threw her arms around him and kissed him. At the press of her lips against his, Mac forgot any other reason he'd come besides embracing this woman and kissing her senseless.

Mac ran his fingers through her hair. He was surprised when all his digits made it through without obstruction. He pulled away and looked at the crown of her head and then at both ears. There was no pen tucked anywhere.

"Do you want to see the centerpieces?" she asked. "If we order them today, we can get the rush shipping. It'll cost a pretty penny, but I think it fits with the base colors you chose."

Lana gave him another tug toward the desk, but Mac pulled her back into his embrace. "We don't have to do this."

"We don't have to do what?" she asked, tilting her head back to gaze at him.

For the first time in years, he had her full attention. This wasn't a break between research projects. Or a stolen moment between fact-checking. Or a quick kiss goodnight before she reopened her laptop and went back to work. She wasn't even working at the moment. She was planning their future together.

"Our wedding doesn't have to be anything fancy," he said.

Now it was Lana who frowned at him. "Who are you, and what have you done with the man I love?"

The laugh escaped his lips before he knew it was there. Mac inhaled a breath of fresh air and got a lungful of coffee and cream.

"You've been dreaming about this day all your life," Lana said. "I want you to have what you want."

"You're what I want," he said. "You're all I've ever wanted. You know that, right? We could elope, and I'd be happy."

Mac pulled away from her. He peered into the mirror over the desk, eyes wide. Putting his hands to his face, he pushed his cheeks around as though he could rearrange his features.

"What are you doing?" she asked.

"Looking to see what I've done with the man you love. He would never say these words."

Lana giggled at his reflection. He grinned back at her. At that moment, his heart filled with so much love for this woman. His friends had been wrong. There was nothing to worry about. Everything was turning out as it should.

"I wanted to talk to you about something," he said.

"What's that?" she asked as she sat down at her computer.

"Where do you want to live after we're married?"

"With you, of course." Lana's grin was cheeky as she clicked a few keys on the keyboard.

Mac came over and rested his hip at the side of the desk. It was a move he'd done many times in their past, but now he didn't feel that he was in competition with the device. "But where would that be?"

Lana looked up at the ceiling as though she were considering the question for the first time. Her hand went to the top of the laptop as though she were going to close it. Then her gaze narrowed on the screen.

"Oh no," she said.

"What?"

"It's the magazine."

Mac's heart skipped a beat. He blinked rapidly, trying to stave off any flashbacks from their last night together before their wedding. "Is it the new job? Did you get it?"

"It's not about the promotion. It's the story."

So, it would be a repeat of the last time. A new story would take her away from him. But why was she looking at her screen with a mix of horror and anger?

"They printed the wrong story," she said.

"What do you mean, the wrong story?"

Mac came to look over her shoulder. He saw the glossy mast of the magazine who had uprooted his life a year ago. The story Lana had accepted at that time had been about cat costumes. The headline on the screen with her byline now read *The Cult of the Purple Rush Brides.*

CHAPTER NINETEEN

"This is not the story that I wrote," Lana said as she looked around the room.

She expected to see eyes narrowed, lips curled, and fingers pointing at her to get out. Most of the residents of the Purple Heart Ranch looked at her with compassion and concern. Many of the women stood, forming a semi-circle around her. But what comforted Lana most, was the man standing at her back.

Mac hadn't said much after reading the story and then driving her here to the ranch. He hadn't left her side for a moment as Dylan Banks gathered the soldiers and their families to hear about the scathing article that defamed their homestead and way of life.

"Well, it is the story that I wrote," Lana said. "My

editor sent me here to tell a story of this place being a cult."

Dylan, whose features had been impassive, tightened as he regarded her. His thumb absentmindedly rubbed at the skin of his wife's neck.

"You gotta admit," Lana said, holding up her hands in her own defense, "on paper, this place is unreal. You each came here and found your perfect match in days. I mean, where else does that happen?"

Lana felt Mac's body warm her back. He'd always said that he'd known she was the one from the first moment he'd laid eyes on her. Lana hadn't felt that way at that moment. But she'd never felt even an ounce of feeling for another living soul that she did for the man who had always been by her side.

Looking out at the crowd of couples, she saw that each man had that same twinkle in his eye when he looked at his wife. Each wife had the calm, confident demeanor of someone who knew they were cared for and would never have a serious worry for the rest of their life.

No, the whole idea of finding that one person in life who you were meant to be with was not so far-fetched.

"That happens here," Lana admitted. "This place is a miracle. You all are so lucky to have found each other. This ranch, and what it is capable of... well, no one would believe the truth of it."

"Yes, they would," said Maggie Banks, holding up a printed sheet of paper. "They would if they read the article you meant to publish."

Lana had printed a number of copies at the motel before rushing over to the ranch. She needed to show them proof of her deeds. But most of the couples hadn't even read it. They appeared to simply take her word for it. Only Maggie and Sarai Cannon had taken one of the copies.

"This is really well written," said Sarai.

Lana took that as a compliment as the woman was a successful blogger. Lana wondered at the freedom to write what she wanted, without waiting for an editor to assign her a story. Or change the story after it was written.

"I'm going to get the magazine to retract it," said Lana.

"There's no need," said Dylan. "If your readers believe what's printed here, then they won't want to visit. That keeps this place clear for those who really need the healing."

"But...they're lies."

Dylan shrugged. The movement was repeated by nearly every person in the room. Lana felt a shudder cross over her own shoulders.

In her short career, Lana hadn't written the most compelling or hard-hitting stories. But they'd always been filled to the brim with facts. It felt wrong to let this story stand as it was.

She turned to look over her shoulder, seeking Mac's support. He still had his hand at her low back. His shoulder bumped hers. But his gaze was out the window. Far off in the distance, she spied the gazebo where they'd be married in just a few days.

"Mac?"

"You're going back, aren't you?" he asked, his gaze still out the window.

"Just for a day. You know I can't let this stand. I'll be back for our wedding. I won't miss that again."

"Are you going to take the promotion?" asked Mac, finally turning his gaze on her.

"What?"

"You got the story. This will be an advancement in your career at the magazine."

Lana set her mouth to say no, but nothing came out. She took a breath and tried again. "After what they did…" She tried to sound indignant. But it came out husky. "I don't know?"

Mac enfolded her into his arms. She collapsed into him, seeking his calm, confident care. All her life, Lana had been fascinated at digging for the truth, uncovering the facts. All which had impacted her ability to take her own real-life story at face value.

She loved this man. She was going to marry him and spend the rest of her life with him. Of that, she was certain. It was a fact.

What she had no idea of was where that left her career?

he bells tinkled as Mac walked into the wedding shop the next morning. Nancy gave him a wave as she tied up another customer's package with a pastel pink bow. Mac liked the woman's company, but he didn't need her help today.

The bell tinkled again as Grizz's large body filled the doorway. His normally stern face looked uncertain as he gazed around at the frills. He wore a cotton camouflage shirt tucked into khakis. His boots pounded the dainty floor, making Mac think the large man would leave cracks behind.

"You really didn't have to come, Grizz," came the trilling voice of his wife.

Grizz held the door open as Patty flitted into the

shop. The petite woman dressed in a light blue sundress looked as though she absolutely belonged in the bridal shop. Just not with her husband.

"This is important to you," Grizz growled. "So, I'm here."

"Well, it is *our* wedding," said Patty.

Grizz shrugged his massive shoulders and then hunched when he saw he was standing near china. "A wedding is just a party."

Both Patty and Mac frowned at that cool assessment. Grizz didn't appear to notice as he sidestepped an arrangement of cake toppers.

"It's a ceremony where the bride and groom make a promise to each other," said Grizz. "I've already made my promise. My focus is on building you a house where we'll raise our family and spend the rest of our lives."

Patty grinned up at him like he hung the moon. Grizz just might be tall enough to reach the rock. He enfolded Patty in his large arms and bent down to meet her kiss.

Behind them, Keaton and Brenda walked in arm in arm. When Keaton saw his sister wrapped up in his best friend's embrace, he groaned.

"You need to get started on that house soon,"

Keaton moaned. "My delicate constitution can't handle you defiling my sister on a daily basis."

Patty broke the kiss and gave her brother a wicked smile. "Sometimes, twice a day."

Keaton made a choked sound and turned for the door. Brenda snaked her hand around his arm and steered him back into the shop.

"Let's get this over with," huffed Keaton. "I've compiled a wedding checklist from two of the most reputable wedding planning sites. This shouldn't take us long."

Brenda pinched the bridge between her nose. Her husband was a planner. Keaton might not like the idea of picking colors and patterns, but now that Mac had helped with that part, it was simply logistics left, which Keaton excelled at.

Brenda shot Mac an imploring glare. Mac chuckled and shook his head. No way was Mac getting anywhere near Keaton when he had his pen and notepad out. Mac had spent enough time with the man in the Army. Mac had gotten out for a reason. At the top of the list was Keaton's notepad.

Mac kept to the sidelines as he watched the two couples consider, bicker, and compromise over wedding plans. This was how it should be; bride and groom working together to plan the day that would start the rest of their lives together.

Mac looked down at his phone. Lana hadn't called. He knew she was likely still on the plane. He still had no idea what she planned to do once she got to her office. He had no idea if she would take the job or tell them to shove it.

Would she even come back to him?

Would she run again?

A text alert beeped on his phone. Mac looked down to see Lana's name.

Just landed.

That was it. No, *I love yous*. No hint of what she was planning to do. No assurance that she would come back to him.

"Mac, you good?" said Keaton.

Mac looked up to see his friends close around him. Keaton and Grizz had closed around him the last time he'd been left at the altar. They'd closed around him each time Lana had turned down his proposal of marriage. They had the look in their eyes that it was happening again.

"Everything all right with Lana?" asked Grizz.

"Yeah," Mac held up his phone as though it were proof. "She just landed."

"When will she be back?" asked Keaton.

Mac had to focus on releasing the tension in his clenched jaw. "This weekend, obviously."

Keaton and Grizz looked at one another, sharing another of their silent, speaking glances.

"She'll be back," Mac insisted.

His friends said nothing.

Mac felt the tension in his chest tighten. His fingers clenched into fists. The walls of the tiny shop began to close in on him.

"Everything good for this weekend?" said Patty, looking up from one of Nancy's pattern books. "You and Lana need a hand with any of your plans?"

"No," said Mac, backing toward the door. "Everything is good. I'm going to go for a walk."

CHAPTER TWENTY-ONE

The clacking on keyboards made Lana wince as she walked into the building. She only just stopped herself from waving her hands in front of her face as though she were warding off a swarm of bees. The red ink on white sheets of paper made her eyes hurt, and she had to squint. The slicing sound of scissors snipping away at images made her hackles rise. And the pace of the people rushing about made her want to keep still.

Back on the ranch, the people and even the animals had all moved slower. No one rushed. No one shouted. Lana rubbed her thumb down her ring finger and was instantly calmed.

"Hunt, you're back," shouted Reyanna from

across the room. "Good. Get in here. I have another story for you."

"Actually…" but Reyanna had already ducked inside her office. Lana ducked and twisted around her colleagues until she was standing before the editor's desk. "I want to talk with you about the last story."

"Great work, Hunt." Reyanna's eyes lit up as she took a swig of her coffee. After she swallowed a grin lit her face. "Our readers are eating it up."

Lana knew the readers would eat up the sensationalized drivel that she'd penned about the Purple Heart Ranch. She'd been hoping to stretch them to eat something more hearty, like the story of healing and strength and love that she'd crafted.

"That wasn't the story I'd hoped to publish," Lana said.

"Oh, I saw the other one," Reyanna frowned into her coffee. "I figured that was the first draft, or you'd gotten stuck watching the Hallmark Channel out in cow country. I didn't even read all the way through it."

"That was the story."

"Cow country?"

"No, the Hallmark Channel. I mean, the touchy-feely story. The article about the strong women and the power of community."

Reyanna studied Lana as though she had grown horns on her head and spots on her chest. "I think there may have been something in that sweet tea you were drinking."

"Sweet tea is a southern drink."

Reyanna's lips paused in a small O with the coffee cup hovering just at her lower lip. "And?"

"Montana is in the Midwest."

"Whatever." Reyanna sat the mug down and ruffled through some papers. Once she found what she wanted, she handed the documents to Lana.

"What's this?" asked Lana.

"The promotion. It's yours."

Lana looked down at the paperwork. It was a contract. At the top of the legalese, in bold, was her new title, Features Writer. There was also a five-digit salary that was closer to six figures than Lana had dared hope. It was everything she'd been working for.

"I need you on this new story," said Reyanna, reclaiming her mug and taking a sip. "There's that reality star, Betsey Blade, who's coming out of rehab."

Lana knew of the star. The woman had been on

television since she was a child on the talent circuit. The public had followed her dating life, her breakups, and now her break down. From all reports, it looked like Betsey was on the up and up.

"You want an exclusive on how she's changing her life around for the better?" asked Lana.

"No." Reyanna downed her last drop of coffee and tossed the container in the trash. "I want you there for when she falls off the wagon again. Our readers will love it."

Lana set the papers down on the edge of the desk. With a light gust of wind, they'd easily fall into the bin atop the empty coffee mug.

"You'll have to be there this weekend," said Reyanna. "I'm sure that won't be a problem."

"I can't this weekend."

"What do you mean you can't?"

"I'm getting married."

Reyanna's brows drew together. "I thought you already were married."

Lana should've already been married. She should've shown up that weekend a year ago. She shouldn't have left Mac this morning.

"I'm getting married on Saturday," said Lana, standing. "And I'm not signing the contract. I'll hand in my resignation before the end of the day."

Lana didn't bother offering Reyanna an explanation. She didn't think the editor would understand the angle of her love story with Mac. Neither did Lana bother clearing her desk. There was nothing there she needed. She had no idea where she'd find another job as a reporter. But she knew for certain that sensationalism wasn't the kind of stories she wanted to tell. She'd figure this out. She and Mac would figure this out together.

She did make a quick run to her home. But she packed light. She could send for this stuff later after she'd settled into life on the ranch. There was just one item that she needed to pack. Then she booked the next flight out.

She couldn't wait to tell Mac. She couldn't wait to see him. She couldn't wait to kiss him. She couldn't wait to spend the rest of her life with him.

CHAPTER TWENTY-TWO

The sun shone done on the gazebo that overlooked the small lake that bordered the Purple Heart Ranch and Vance Ranch. Woven around the structure were flowers of blushing pink and ripe plum. The flowers had come in last night, and Mac finished arranging them early this morning. The chairs were set. The altar in place. All that was missing was the bride.

It was nearing forty-eight hours since she'd left, and Lana hadn't called. She hadn't texted since she'd told him that she'd landed. That was two days ago. Mac's phone sat restless and silent in his back pocket.

He stood before the gazebo, where they were to be married later this afternoon. He tilted his face up to the sun, trying to blind the flashbacks from the last time he found himself in this predicament.

Perhaps it was the sun that did the trick. The bright lights washed out the memories of that day. The shinning rays slid down his throat, leaving a hollowness in his chest. Mac was numb in the warmth.

For his first wedding day, Mac had had time to let everyone know that Lana wasn't coming. This time, he only had hours. He didn't move. He took a few minutes to let that sink in.

She wasn't coming.

The sun was higher in the sky now. There was a light breeze picking up. The day was a bit overcast. It looked like rain would threaten.

And still, his cellphone was silent. Not a word. Again.

She wasn't coming.

There was a part of Mac that worried that something had gone wrong. Could she be somewhere hurt? But he knew in his heart that Lana was fine. He could sense in his heart that, once again, she'd made her decision.

She wasn't coming.

Mac would not wait for her. He could no longer hope that this next time when he chased after her, things would be different. Because everything was the same. He was standing at the altar, and she was not coming.

"Here early, I see?" said Pastor Vance.

Mac had never been much of a religious guy. Sure, he went to church on the requisite holidays when he was with his family. He was always in the pews on Sundays during his summers with his grandparents. But other than that, he had little to no interaction with pastors.

Pastor Vance was different. For one, the man was the same age as Mac. He still had all his hair and teeth and didn't spend any time shouting down at Mac with a disapproving glare in his narrowed gaze. Every other word out of Walter's mouth wasn't a prayer or biblical verse, even though he carried a black Bible in his hand. The man was the most down to earth, practical, and patient man Mac had ever met. It was a shame he wouldn't be delivering Mac's vows.

"I don't think there's going to be a wedding today," Mac admitted. "I seem to have misplaced my bride."

Vance pursed his lips. He took a deep inhale through his flaring nostrils as he regarded the purple and pink decorations.

"I don't think Lana wants to get married."

"No?" said Vance. "It sure looked to me that she did that night she proposed to you."

It had looked to Mac that she did as well. He thought he'd done everything right this time. He hadn't pushed or prodded. He'd let her take the lead. So, how had he ended up back alone before an altar?

"Is this about the article that she wrote?" asked Pastor Vance.

Mac didn't answer. He'd read the original article, the scathing exposé full of misdirections and half-truths. When he'd seen those words, Mac had feared Lana had grown into a stranger who he wouldn't be able to respect.

Then he read the second draft. There, in the metaphors and prose she'd penned about strength and courage, was the woman he loved, the writer who should be winning awards. The writer he thought she wanted to be. But if that revision wasn't going to get her promoted, would she revert to the original draft?

"I have a feeling the story is not over for you two," said Pastor Vance. "Plus, I placed a bet that this wedding would be happening today."

Mac wanted to laugh, but his chest felt too constricted. The betting pool about who would get wed and when in this town was a true racket. Mac wondered what the odds on him and Lana had been? Whatever the odds, it looked like neither he nor Pastor Vance would win today.

He looked around at all his decorations, all his plans. He had wanted the wedding of his dreams. But at the end of the day, all that had truly mattered to him was that he had his dream girl at his side. His heart ached because he knew that he would go through this all again if Lana hinted at even a glimmer of hope that they could be together.

Lana Hunt was a part of him, his heart, his soul. There would never be another woman for him.

The sun had reached higher in the sky. Guests would be arriving soon. And she still hadn't called.

Because she wasn't coming.

CHAPTER TWENTY-THREE

he moment the Unfasten Your Seatbelt light went off, Lana shot out of her chair. She didn't have time to count to ten and wait for the kid beside her to wiggle his way out of his seat. She didn't have the patience to take deep breaths when the pregnant woman across the aisle waddled to standing.

From her economy seat in the middle of the plane, Lana wanted to shout that it was her wedding day, and she was going to be late. Though it was clear to everyone there that that might be the case. Lana had stopped home to grab one item; her wedding dress from a year ago. It was now rumpled from sitting in the middle seat for eight hours.

When she'd boarded the plane last night, they'd

had to be diverted after a passenger had a heart attack thirty minutes after takeoff. They sat on the tarmac for another few hours before being cleared for take-off again. Only to have a mechanical issue while they were taxiing.

Back to the terminal they went to deplane. By then, Lana's cell phone was dead. She'd rooted in her bag for her charger, but it wasn't there. Had she even packed it when she left the motel? She knew she had an extra back at her desk at *ChatterZine*, but that wasn't her desk anymore.

While sitting in the stalled plane earlier, Lana had decided she was going to go freelance. Either she was going to write the stories that meant something, or she wasn't going to write at all. Right now, she was pretty sure her first report would be a scathing piece on the perils of domestic air travel.

By the time she got booked on a new flight, it was the next day. The shops with cell phone charges were opening their doors just as the voice over the intercom called to announce that her flight was boarding. Weighing her odds, Lana decided to grab her seat rather than grabbing a charger.

Mac would wait for her. He always waited for her. And she was coming for him. Though she was cutting it close.

Halfway through the flight, Lana rose from her middle seat, stepped over the wiggling kid, grabbed her carry on from the overhead compartment, and headed to the bathroom. Once she hit the ground, she would have no time to spare, so she dressed for the part she wanted most in life.

The entire plane stopped and stared when she emerged in her wedding gown.

As a reporter, Lana had always tried to blend into the background of her writing. She wanted the facts to shine. But today, the fact was that she was getting married to the man she'd loved for more than half her life. Today, she was finally writing the story she was meant to tell.

If she could just get off this blasted plane!

Racing through arrivals in pumps, her suitcase rolling in pace behind her, Lana finally reached the parking terminal where she'd left her rental car. Her phone was still dead. Time was ticking away.

She knew Mac would be beside himself. She just had to hope he believed in their love enough, believed in her enough, to wait just one more hour.

Lana tore out of the parking lot and onto the highway. It was a short drive to the ranch. Soon, the long stretch of highway narrowed into a two-lane road with pastures as far as the eye could see. The sight was a far cry from the concrete city she'd been in just two days ago. Something in Lana settled as the green and brown zoomed past her. There was still a sense of urgency to get to Mac, but the heaviness that hung over her shoulders sank down into the seat.

Just a few more miles, and she saw the sign for The Purple Heart Ranch. She made her way into the welcoming gate, passing the pastel flowers that were in full bloom. She drove the car down the dirt path that led right to the gazebo, where she would say her vows to the man she could no longer spend a single day without. She had expected a small crowd gathered. Instead, she saw Keaton and Grizz dismantling the decorations.

"Stop that," Lana said, hopping out of the car.

The two men looked at her agape, their mouths hung open, their gazes going wide. Then they looked at each other. First Keaton's brows raised, arching high as though forming a question. In answer, Grizz lowered one brow in a grimace. Around them, the purple and pink streamers that they had been pulling down hung limp in the silence.

"Why do you look so surprised?" Lana demanded. She didn't wait for their answer. "Where is everyone? Where is Mac?"

"Mac is back at the ranch packing," said Keaton.

"Packing?" said Lana. "To go where?"

Neither man answered. They just exchanged another of those speaking glances between themselves.

"We're supposed to be getting married," said Lana.

"You're running a little late," said Keaton, coming down the gazebo stairs. "We thought you weren't coming. Can you blame us?"

"Am I never going to live that down with you two?" Lana looked between Mac's two best friends. They'd never had this out. Now was as good a time as ever. "You two know how he is. His parents named him Mac for a reason. He can be just like a Mack truck when there's something he wants."

"No one forced you, Lana," said Grizz.

"No," Lana agreed. "That's the point. I had to fight to have a say in my own relationship. Mac decided we were gonna be friends, and then date, and then get married. He just sped along, and I was expected to—what? Sit quietly, and enjoy the ride?"

The two men shared another of those glances. But there were no eyebrow questions raised this time. Both Keaton and Grizz pursed their lips as they regarded one another, as though they were actually hearing what Lana had to say.

"I told Mac no so many times because I wasn't ready when he was."

"But you are today?" asked Grizz.

Now it was Lana who raised her brow in answer to his question. To make sure they understood her point, she pursed her lips and gave a decisive nod of her head.

Grizz relaxed his shoulders. But Keaton was still tense.

"What about the job?" asked Keaton.

"They offered me the promotion," Lana said. "But, they've driven me toward places I didn't want to go in my writing. So, I quit."

When Lana looked up, she saw something she never thought she'd see. Grizz's mouth was stretched wide in a rare smile. Keaton rubbed at his chin with a thoughtful look on his face. It wasn't exactly a smile, but it was close enough.

"Come on," said Keaton. "We'll give you a ride."

CHAPTER TWENTY-FOUR

*M*ac looked at his reflection in the mirror. The man staring back at him looked tired but determined. Behind him, he spied the tux jacket he'd picked out for his wedding today. Instead of tossing it into the suitcase that was open on the bed, Mac reached over and shoved the jacket in a bag for donations along with the collared shirt, tie, and pants he'd planned to wear today. It wasn't likely he'd ever wear the things.

He sat the bag of donations down on the floor next to the trash bin. On the bedside table, he saw the wedding planner book he'd had for years. The binder page opened to patterns featuring the colors he'd chose so long ago. The blush and plum really were the best colors for him and Lana. Two things that you wouldn't think go together, but complemented each other when side by side.

Mac closed the book. It was used so it wouldn't go in with the donations. Instead, he dropped the now useless book into the trash bin.

What was between those pages no longer mattered. Not when the woman who had stolen his heart wasn't invested in the story there. Mac was finally facing facts. Pressuring Lana Hunt to do something when she wasn't ready was a recipe for disaster. The only thing that had ever worked was waiting until she was ready.

Mac heaved a heavy sigh as he closed his suitcase. He'd waited more than half of his life for this woman. He had no doubt he would continue waiting for the rest of it. It was his only choice because he knew that he would love her every day that he drew breath on this earth.

The sound of something tapping on glass brought his attention around. Mac glanced up first into the mirror before him. He had to blink a few times to be certain he was seeing what he thought he was seeing. Still not trusting his eyes, he whirled around to look directly at the window.

And there she was.

Lana was outside his window. Her hair was a

bird's nest of a mess. Her makeup was smudged at every corner of her eyes. There were bags above her cheeks as though she hadn't slept all night. But all of those details paled in comparison to the most glaring detail.

When she stepped over the windowsill, Lana stood in a wedding dress. But not just any wedding dress. It was the wedding dress they'd picked out last year. And, despite the mess of her hair and makeup, she looked breathtakingly beautiful.

"Hi," she said, out of breath.

"Hey," he said. Mac had trouble forcing the word out. His eyes were so wide on his face, they made it tough for his mouth to open and form words.

"Can I come in?" she asked.

The question was a moot point as she was already inside. Mac was able to nod his head. Any further words eluded him.

He'd thought she wasn't coming. He'd thought the wedding was off. But there she stood, on the day of their second wedding, looking stunningly disheveled in the dress meant for their first time.

"I'm late," she said.

Again, Mac could only nod.

"I would've called, but there was a heart attack, and no charger, and then the plane broke."

The words coming from her mouth made no sense. It didn't matter much to Mac. He couldn't move his gaze from her lips. He wondered if, when they stopped, if he could kiss her. Signs pointed to probably since she had climbed into his window in a wedding dress on their wedding day.

Lana wrung her hands as she worried her lips. Her thumb rubbed back and forth over the engagement ring on her finger. She looked worried and unsure of herself. Two things that Mac didn't identify with this strong woman.

"You're leaving?" she asked.

Mac blinked, taking his gaze from her mouth and lifting it to her eyes. Lana wasn't looking at him. She was looking behind him at the suitcase on his bed.

"Yeah," he said.

"Mac, please don't." Her face crumpled and tears glistened at the corners of her eyes.

Mac had her in his arms in an instant. The sob that escaped her lips pierced his heart. He tucked Lana under his chin so that her cheek rested right against his chest. That feeling of clicking sounded all throughout his body. Mac recognized the sound as gears fitting together and not a clock that he needed to rush. He would give Lana all the time she needed until she was ready to be with him.

"Please, don't give up on me, Mac."

Give up on her? Where did that come from?

"I quit. I quit *ChatterZine*."

"Why would you do that?" he asked. "You loved that job."

"No, I love you," she said. "I may have figured this out late, but I figured it out. I've been chasing other peoples' stories for so long that I didn't stop to look at my own. It's you. You're my story. My beginning, my middle, my end. The facts of my life don't make sense without you in it."

Mac's lids lowered as he listened to Lana's heartfelt truth. His mouth had gone slack from her confession. So, he still had trouble making any coherent words.

Lana pulled away from him, looking up at him with tear-filled eyes. "Please, don't leave. Stay and give me another chance."

Mac lifted his hand to wipe at the tear trailing down her face. His fingers shook as he did so. "I was leaving the ranch to come to you."

Lana blinked. And then blinked a few times again as though the words weren't coming into focus. "You were coming for me?"

"Of course, I was coming for you. I always come for you."

She blinked a few more times. Slowly now, as though everything was coming clear. Then, without warning, she reached up to him and pulled him down to her lips.

Lana's kiss was bruising, claiming. Mac had no trouble following her lead. He would follow this woman to the ends of the earth.

"You still want to marry me?" she asked when they came up for air, her voice breathless.

"I told you when we were six; you're the only girl for me, Lana Hunt."

Her smile was so bright it dried the tears in her eyes. Then she nodded, her features going business-like. Stepping away from him, she reached up to her hair, where she usually kept a pen. Finding none there, she looked around his room.

"We can start planning for our third and final wedding." She grabbed a stub of a pencil and an old receipt from his bedside table. "We can make it as big and grand as you want. We can invite as many people. No expense will be spared. And I will be there by your side, planning every color, every place setting, everything."

Mac took the pencil and scrap of paper from her hand. "We don't need a new date. We can do it now."

"Keaton and Grizz pulled all the decorations down and—"

"None of that matters," he said. "All that matters is the promise we make to each other to always come for each other for the rest of our lives."

Lana leaned her forehead against Mac. She sighed a deep, contented sigh as she said, "I promise you that."

"I promise you, too." Mac bent his head and sealed that solemn vow with a gentle kiss. "But, I do want this made legal, so..."

Mac pulled away from Lana. He took the few steps to his bedroom door. Turning the knob, he prepared to shout downstairs. But when he opened the door, he saw that there was no need.

Brenda and Keaton, Patty and Grizz, Porco, Rusty, and Spinelli all stood in the upstairs hall. Mac looked beyond them to see Pastor Vance leaning against the railing, Bible in hand.

"Pastor Vance, you said if we needed you?"

The pastor made his way forward, an expectant smile on his face. "It sounded to me like the two of you got through the important parts. I couldn't have written any better vows myself. All that's left for me to do is pronounce you man and wife."

Mac turned back to Lana in her crumpled wedding dress. He was barefoot and in jeans and a t-shirt. It might not be the wedding he'd planned, but it fulfilled his every dream.

"Hot, hot, hot!"

David Porco tossed the sizzling piece of bacon from one hand to another. The grease singed the fingers of first his right and then left hand, and so he popped the strip of sweet meat into his mouth.

"Ow -hot." Chew. "Hiss -hot." Chew.

"What do you expect, Porco?" said Mac. "You pulled it straight out of the frying pan."

"Worth it," said Porco. Bacon was his first love. It had narrowly won that position after a long hard-fought battle with honeyed ham. Though Porco often cheated on bacon and ham with pork chops. A little bit of fire was nothing to keep the man from his calling.

Mac shook his head as he regarded his friend, but he smiled as he sipped at his steaming cup of coffee. His gaze didn't linger for long on Porco. It slid to his wife.

Lana Kenzie's head was down, her gaze focused on her notepad. The cup of coffee at her side had long gone tepid. The two were preparing to leave for their honeymoon in just a few hours. Which was why Lana's attention was on her pad.

"You need to hurry and finish that story," said Mac, toying with the pen tucked behind her ear. "We agreed you would not be working on our honeymoon."

Lana tore her gaze away from her words and gazed adoringly at her husband. "Don't worry, I won't. I just need to fix the ending before I submit it. Then I'm all yours."

"You've always been all mine." Mac went in and nipped her lower lip for a kiss.

Porco grabbed another strip of bacon from the pan. He had to repeat the tossing of the sizzling meat from hand to hand again. He allowed this strip to cool as he walked out the back door of the house.

The big house was filled with newlyweds kissing and canoodling in every corner. Porco was thankful he lived across the field in one of the bungalows typically inhabited by the ranch hands. He, Spinelli, and Rusty took up the rooms in the three-bedroom domicile. But Porco had to keep coming back to the big house; it's where all the food was.

He didn't mind maneuvering around embracing couples to get to the fridge. He had every hope that he would be an obnoxious, embracing newlywed someday soon. He just had to find her first.

Since he'd come to this town, he'd begun looking in earnest since he planned to stay here for many years. He was ready to settle down. He just needed to find the right girl, the one who had that certain spark.

"This is absolute manure!"

Porco turned to see Brenda storming his way. Her husband and brother in tow.

Keaton looked down at a stack of papers with concern on his brow. Pastor Vance looked as though he was praying for patience.

"Just who does he think he is to tell me what I can and can't put on my lands," said Brenda.

"Well, Bren," said Vance, "it could just be a huge missed steak."

Brenda's green eyes flared. Keaton winced and gave his brother in a law a subtle shake of the head.

"You know," said the pastor. "Because they're

vegans and you're a cattle rancher. I'm just trying to lighten the mood."

"What's going on?" Porco sidled up beside Keaton, giving the siblings a wide berth.

"It's the neighbors again," said Keaton.

As far as Porco knew, the neighbors to the Vance Ranch were the Purple Heart Ranch next door. The two ranches got along fine, often hosting barbecues on each other's land.

"The commune vegan commune next door," Keaton clarified. "They've filed an injunction to try and stop Bren from spraying fertilizer on the pasture that borders their land. Apparently, they're trying to get an organic certification for their vegetables."

Porco turned his nose up at the mention of the word vegetables. He didn't see the need for the food group. Cows and pigs ate grass. He ate their meat. Therefore, he got a daily dose of vegetables.

Too bad his parents had never bought into that argument and kept putting broccoli and carrots on his plate.

"I'm going to fight this, Walter," Brenda was saying. "I've been playing nice for too long. If it's a feud those overgrown flower children want, it's a feud they'll get."

Brenda stormed off. Heaving deep sighs, Walter

and Keaton trudged after her. Porco held back. He pitied anyone who stood in that woman's way. He'd seen Brenda square off against a bull. It was the bull who took a step back. Whoever these vegetable farmers were, he did not envy them. Especially, if they grew the hated foodstuffs.

Porco popped the last piece of bacon in his mouth. He headed in the opposite direction. He had a date to get ready for. Maybe tonight he'd finally feel that spark that told him that the woman across from him was the one.

Porco had felt plenty of tingles with the women he'd dated over the past few weeks. The girl he'd be seeing tonight had a fire inside her, and she'd left him feeling warm after their last date. Who knew? Maybe Rosalind would turn out to be the one for him.

Rosalind is not the one for this Romeo.
Porco is about to get his first sight of the girl next door.
Her name is Jules.
She's one of those overgrown flower children who live on the organic, vegan farm next door.

She grows soybeans, loves vegetable dishes, ...and has a pet pig.
Order your copy of
The Rancher takes his Star Crossed Love today!

Shanae Johnson was raised by Saturday Morning cartoons and After School Specials. She still doesn't understand why there isn't a life lesson that ties the issues of the day together just before bedtime. While she's still waiting for the meaning of it all, she writes stories to try and figure it all out. Her books are wholesome and sweet, but her are heroes are hot and heroines are full of sass!

And by the way, the E elongates the A. So it's pronounced Shan-aaaaaaaa. Perfect for a hero to call out across the moors, or up to a balcony, or to blare outside her window on a boombox. If you hear him calling her name, please send him her way!

You can sign up for Shanae's Reader Group at http://bit.ly/ShanaeJohnsonReaders

Also By Shanae Johnson

The Rangers of Purple Heart

The Rancher takes his Convenient Bride

The Rancher takes his Best Friend's Sister

The Rancher takes his Runaway Bride

The Rancher takes his Star Crossed Love

The Rancher takes his Love at First Sight

The Rancher takes his Last Chance at Love

The Brides of Purple Heart

On His Bended Knee

Hand Over His Heart

Offering His Arm

His Permanent Scar

Having His Back

In Over His Head

Always On His Mind

Every Step He Takes

In His Good Hands

Light Up His Life

Strength to Stand

The Rebel Royals series

The King and the Kindergarten Teacher

The Prince and the Pie Maker

The Duke and the DJ

The Marquis and the Magician's Assistant

The Princess and the Principal